ALL FOR

MY

LOVE

Clove Friday

PUBLISHING HOUSE
2021

CONTENTS

CHAPTER ONE

I can't believe he didn't want to come, Tia thought as she stood in line at the 7-Eleven. *I get so tired of going places by myself, especially with this crowd that I'm meeting tonight.*

Tia was comfortable, and more than that, she was accustomed to going places without her husband Carl. But this group of people could not seem to understand how or why Tia was out alone so often. They are going to have questions, they are going to cause her to make excuses, and they are going to talk about Tia *and* her marriage after she is gone.

Why couldn't he just come along, she thought. These were Carl's friends, or more accurately, Carl's associates. He brought them into the marriage, and they were *okay,* so Tia tried to deal with them. However, when Carl and Tia were alone, she called the group "The Nerds". Carl even began to call them that when he spoke about the bunch.

Dominique, one of Carl's ex-coworkers, put together a Sunday Affair and his wife, Janice, had given Tia two tickets. *Obviously, Janice expected me to come with Carl because she gave me a pair of tickets*; Tia continued to upset herself by thinking about how inconsiderate Carl had been. *They would be thrown totally off balance if I came up in there with one of my girls; and I would definitely*

1

be an outcast if I brought one of my male friends, Tia was thinking when the line moved her back into reality.

When Tia looked up, she was surprised to see that the person who had been holding up the line buying $500,000.00 worth of lottery tickets was a handsome, dark skinned brother. He looked just as surprised when he turned, to see that she had been standing behind him, unnoticed, the whole time.

As he walked out, Tia noticed that there was something about the bottom half of his body that she didn't quite like. Maybe his pants were too tight or too short; maybe it was his shoes. *Well, I would've still given him the eye if I had seen him sooner; he was cute*, Tia thought, *too late*. Although she was married, Tia still flirted innocently. *Thinking about Carl and his issues is fucking with my cutie radar*. Tia smiled at her thoughts as she paid for the mints that she stopped to get. As Tia walked to her Lexus, she thought again about her lease. It would end next month, and she had not decided what she was going to do about a vehicle. "Excuse me", she heard.

Tia looked up into the Range Rover that had pulled up next to her to find who she knew *better* be this week's lotto winner. "Are you married?", he asked as Tia unarmed her alarm to get inside her SUV.

She simply smiled and showed him her ring finger on which she wore a very modest wedding ring. Tia was surprised first that he was there and secondly that he was better looking than she thought. Tia picked up her cell phone before she even closed her door; she wanted to call someone and vent.

"Can you have friends?", she heard him say while thinking about who she wanted to talk to.

"Sure." she said. "What's your name?" she asked, maybe sounding a little *too* friendly.

"Shun", he said.

"Sean?", Tia asked. Did she hear an accent?

"Yeah. What's yours?", the cutie with the accent asked.

"Tia", she said. *I should have known he was a foreigner,* she thought, answering the question for herself as to why she hadn't seen him before.

Cutie, or "Shun", must have noticed that Tia was no longer interested and said, "Why don't you take my number."

"What is it?", Tia asked with her cell phone in hand. She put Sean's number in when he gave it to her and began to drive off. She decided that she could at least wave goodbye. When she turned and waved, Sean gave her the hand to the side of the face signal with the thumb up and the pinky sticking out. Tia knew that sign meant to call now.

What the heck, Tia thought. *I can't think of anyone that I feel like talking to right now anyway. Why not talk to Sean until I get to where I'm going,* she thought to herself while she pressed the send button.

Tia ended up talking to Sean for two hours. She couldn't believe the time. *Whew,* she thought, *that came out of nowhere.* The conversation just took off. They started off talking about why a married woman would be going to a social function alone and ended up talking about soulmates, traveling, and the craziest things that each had ever done.

Chapter Two

Sean had spent almost two hours talking to Tia. He had hoped that the conversation would be interesting enough to hold his attention while he drove home. But he had been home, sitting in his garage, cell phone to his ear for at least an hour and fifteen minutes now.

He didn't know what possessed him to wait for her outside of 7-Eleven or to actually say something to her. She was attractive, but Sean was accustomed to seeing beautiful women on the regular. Now he surprised himself again with the twinge of disappointment he felt when Tia told him that she had to go. "Send me the email. I'll probably be online for a while tonight," is what she said.

"Definitely. What are you doing tomorrow?" Sean replied, feeling a little out of place.

"I don't know. Call me, or I'll call you. If I don't answer, leave a message and I'll call you back", Tia replied nonchalantly.

"Okay, nice —"

"Bye", Tia said quickly, cutting Sean off mid-sentence. Sean's phone went dead silent.

Sean just sat in his Range Rover for a minute thinking about the conversation that he just had. *She can't be from around here,* he thought, *and she can't be happily married either.*

"Whatever", Sean said aloud as he opened the door to the truck. He had pulled in and parked the Range Rover in between his new G Wagon and high-powered pick-up truck that still had the two Suzuki jet skis attached to the back of it. He had taken his kids jet skiing yesterday and hadn't taken the hitch off the truck yet. *Tomorrow,* he thought as he walked into his beautiful home.

Sean was what could be called self-made. A born hustler, Sean had used the hard-core knowledge acquired from the streets to his advantage and made a substantial life for himself. Everything he touched seemed to turn to gold.

However, Sean's accomplishments as an entrepreneur made his deficiency in his personal life even more apparent. As a man, Sean felt like a failure. He felt that with all his material wealth, his life should be more fulfilled. Instead, he was bored, he was lonely, and the irony of it all was that Sean was married to someone that he originally thought he would live happily ever after with.

CHAPTER THREE

C arl put his son Carlton into his bed and turned to go
downstairs. He had already made sure Tianna was
snuggled into her bed. She was watching the last few minutes
of one of their kiddie shows before she was supposed to turn
the TV off and go to sleep. Now it was Carl's time to relax.

He plopped down in his favorite spot on the sofa and
turned the channel to CNN News. This was his favorite
pastime, and he could not understand why his wife, Tia, had
a problem with it.

Carl allowed Tia to basically come and go as she pleased
without any complaints from him, although she would
probably do the same even if he did complain. *I don't bother her
about what she does*, Carl thought, as he moved a pillow to get
comfortable. *Why does she have to drag me around with her? That's
her thing not mine and I never even pretended to be a social butterfly.*
Carl tried to listen to the news being reported on the riots in
Baltimore, but his thoughts kept going back to his wife.

Carl was startled by the phone and answered without
even realizing that he had fallen asleep. "Hello?"

"What's up man?" Dominique screamed. "What
happened to you guys, Jan said that y'all were comin
through?"

"What man?" Carl was confused. "Didn't Tia tell you that I was home with the kids?"

"Shit was kinda thick, man", Carl heard someone say to Nique. "You gone have to do this more often, and next time I *will be* solo. Hey, what's up with Jan's girl?", the man attempted a whisper.

"Go head on, negro", Dominique chuckled, and Carl could hear him gloat through the phone line.

"Yeah man, you guys coulda came out to show a brotha some love. What happened?" Nique sounded genuinely disappointed.

"What's up? What's up?" Dominique yelled to someone else without giving Carl a chance to reply. "Hey man, I'll see you at the gym tomorrow. These fools ain't leaving." Dominique said, gloating again and relieving Carl of the task of searching for an answer.

"Alright", said Carl and he quickly hung up.

Carl was puzzled. Tia was supposed to be there and from what Nique said, she wasn't. Carl checked the caller ID to make sure his wife hadn't called while he dozed. Nope.

Although it wasn't late, Tia had been gone for quite a while and Carl wondered why she hadn't called if she wasn't where she said she would be.

Carl sat back and tried to listen to Sharpton break down the riot situation but could not help thinking about Tia. He hoped nothing happened to her, but he knew that Tia could handle her own. She wasn't the dainty fragile type at all. She never really *needed* his help but accepted it because she felt he owed it to her.

An hour and a half after talking to Dominique, Carl could take no more. He picked up the phone and dialed his wife's cell phone number.

"Hey." She answered on the first ring.

"What's up?" Carl asked, relieved by her casual tone.

"Nothing. I'm right down the street. I'll be home in a minute." Tia said nicely. "What's up?"

"Nothing's up...just thinking about you. I'll see you when you get here." Carl was taken aback by the coolness in Tia's voice.

"Alright." Tia hung up.

Carl placed the phone in its cradle, closed his eyes and rested his head on the back of the overstuffed leather sofa that he loved but would have never bought without Tia's sales pitch. Tia persuaded Carl to buy the overpriced piece by telling him that they would never have to spend money on furniture again. She said that they would have the sofa forever and that it was *made* to last a lifetime which is why it came with such a high ticket. The speech worked and Carl gave in to his wife's desires, although reluctant, and he has not regretted it yet.

I guess quality is important, Carl thought. He could not remember ever feeling as comfortable on any of the ten living rooms sets that came through his mother's house while he was growing up or any of the five that have been there since he moved out.

Carl heard Tia pull up. He sat up and put his game face on to listen to whatever story Tia was going to give him. Maybe Tia wouldn't bother to give Carl a story at all. Maybe Tia didn't even know that Carl knew she never made it to Dominique's gig. She may not know that Carl knew *already*, but Tia knew that Carl would eventually find out. And if Carl knew his wife, he knew that she already had an explanation prepared.

This has got to be the most unpredictable woman in the world, Carl thought to himself as Tia stretched out across their extra-long, extra comfortable leather sofa with her head in his lap. *I was all worked up after the call from Nique. I really don't even know why,* Carl thought, *Tia is notorious for doing the opposite of what I expect.*

Like tonight, Carl mused, *for some reason I thought it was going to be drama. My baby came in the house, looking sexy as hell (I guess I didn't see her before she left.) She left her shoes right at the front door, which I hate, but not before I noticed that they were new, and I liked them. They were the perfect shoes for the little dress Tia was wearing that also looked new.* Carl's thought diverted to the $1,000 that he could not account for that was missing from his checking account.

Mrs. Tia Lawson can spend some money, Carl reminded himself. He thought about the nice little nest egg that he had when he met his wife. His plan was to at least double it within their first five years of marriage. Carl began to feel a twinge of depression and tried to stop thinking about what he could not change. *I guess my boo had a better plan,* Carl's spirit lightened, and he smiled, *to deplete my shit within the first five years of marriage.*

Carl had come from a long line of worriers, and the curse did not miss him. However, it was difficult for him to dwell on something as trivial as money with Tia lying there so peacefully and looking so angelic.

From the moment Carl saw Tia bend to take those Manolo Blahnik shoes (that he hoped she had at least found on sale somewhere with one of her shopping buddies) off, he knew that he would not be able to front tonight. Carl loved his wife more than anything, but he did not want her to know how much she meant to him.

9

Carl's mother had taught her two sons well. She taught them to work hard to get what they want. She taught them to always be in control of themselves and their things; wives and children included. She also taught them that "It is best to marry someone who loves you more than you love them so you won't be running around like a fool, cause I can't stand no henpecked man", and those were her exact words.

Sorry mama, Carl mentally apologized, as he bent to place a gentle kiss on his wife's lips. Tia sighed and gave her best attempt at a pucker, but she was on the brink of unconsciousness. That did not stop Carl from his quest. He kissed Tia from her head to her perfectly polished toes. Carl dedicated that night to making Tia feel as special and as beautiful as she looked.

CHAPTER FOUR

Tia could not help cracking up at her boss/her boy as she sat in front of her computer trying extremely hard to ignore him.

"What's up? What's up, Mack Mama?" Ken said as he walked past Tia's office.

When Tia didn't answer, Ken stopped midstride and backed up.

"Oh, don't play me like I'm one of those cats sweatin'. I know what you workin' wit," Ken said with a smirk that Tia knew too well. The one Ken wore when he thought he had one up on someone. "Two kids and a husband," Ken finished falling out laughing at his own version of humor.

Because Tia contained herself and was able to hide her smile behind her computer, Ken didn't know he already had her going, so he kept pushing.

"Fallin' all up on *my* set without warnin', wearin' some high priced get up that your husband has no idea he paid for, talkin' and actin' like you The Queen Bee. Negro don't you know I will pull out my wallet sized family photo of the *real* you the next time you try to front on me. You better speak to me this mornin'."

Tia had been trying to get that picture back from Ken ever since Carl had given it to him at the house one Saturday. "Ken is my boy and all, but a family portrait is for family members only. I don't even walk around with one in my wallet," Tia tried to explain to Carl.

Ken and Tia had been friends since college when Tia dated Ken's roommate, Dennis Feldman. Tia and Dennis had a two-year relationship that ended a little before Tia wanted it to end. This was Tia's first real heartbreak, and she was devastated. Tia poured her heart out onto paper to make Dennis understand why he *couldn't* break up with her. She got Ken to deliver the letter to his roommate. Big mistake. Ken read the letter before giving it to Dennis. The letter got passed through their whole chapter of frat brothers before it finally reached the intended recipient.

Since then, Ken had called on Tia to write everything from term papers to business proposals for him. After Tia got over her embarrassment, she didn't mind helping Ken out when he needed her. She put his thoughts on paper for him and they became confidants. He pretended that he felt obligated because of his initial betrayal, but he really enjoyed the way Tia respected his opinion and valued his advice and he appreciated the same from her.

Ken couldn't believe his eyes when Tia walked into *Christopher's*. In fact, he was wondering who the fine honey was that was walking in his direction, with her eyes right on him as if he was expecting her. He was a little disappointed when he realized it was his "Ace Boon Coon", Tia.

"What's up, Boo?" Tia asked just before she brushed Ken's cheek with a kiss. She knew that Ken was shocked speechless, so she added, "I just thought I would stop by to check your new spot out."

Ken still had not said a word when his boy walked over and said "Hey, what's up?" while giving Tia the once over.

"Hi", Tia said and turned back to Ken who still had his mouth open but hadn't said a word.

Ken's friend motioned for the bartender. He noticed that Ken's Henn was low and ordered two on the rocks when the bartender arrived. "What you drinking, Babe?" the friend asked while trying to size up the situation.

"I'll have an Appletini, thank you" Tia replied and noticed that she *was* standing between Ken's legs and could be cock blocking. She took a step back and gently patted Ken's face saying, "Hell-ooooo, what is your rude ass problem? At least acknowledge my presence so I can walk away without causing a scene."

"Tia?", Ken finally said, only half faking the question and he began looking around as if he were looking for someone else.

"Don't play, Fool", Tia said realizing that Ken was insinuating that he couldn't believe it was her.

The bartender had come and placed the three drinks on the bar and Ken's friend raised Tia's drink to hand it to her. When Tia took the drink, she looked up to signal another thanks and realized that it was Charles. She hadn't paid any attention to him before because of Ken's crazy ass, but this was Charles, not a friend, but Ken's brother!

Obviously, Charles had assessed the relationship as being platonic because he seemed to be in hunt mode. That is when he realized that he had seen Tia before. "You look familiar. Have we met?" Charles asked smoothly.

Tia had to concentrate to keep the calm cool attitude that she walked in with. "Yes, we have, *Charles,* on several occasions." Tia answered as cool as a cucumber. "I guess *that's* why little brother here didn't bother with the introductions." Tia elbowed Ken hard enough to bring him into the conversation.

"Man, this is Tia. *I* almost didn't know who she was; you see I'm still sitting here trying to figure out what's going on. I didn't know she was allowed out after dark without her spouse." Ken had unintentionally embarrassed Tia, but he was being honest.

Ken and Tia use to hang all the time before she got married. This would have been one of those spots where if he came in without her or vice versa, everyone they knew would have been asking where the other one was. Ken missed that part of their friendship, but never found it appropriate to mention it.

"Daaamn! Tia? You looking good. I didn't know you still lived here.

How's everything?" Charles said.

"Thanks, yep I'm still here. I've just been on the low. Everything's good, I guess."

The two of them talked for the rest of the evening, leaving Ken to wonder what Tia was doing out alone *and* looking like the *old* Tia. The before marriage Tia, the it's *all about me,* Tia, the Tia that had his friends asking if he was hitting it and wondering *why* he wasn't.

Tia was surprised at how the evening had turned out. She was three for three. Cutie from 7-Eleven seemed to be interesting if nothing else. Ken's spot was "the spot" for real (and charming ass Charles didn't hurt the atmosphere *at all*). When Tia got home, Carl put the icing on the cake with the slow, passionate, tender love waiting when she got in the door. Although Tia had been tipsy and on the verge of slumber, she could still remember how lovingly Carl had placed each kiss down the length of her body.

It was almost 3:00 and Tia was still somewhere between work and La La Land. She had been sitting at her desk all day but had not completed anything because her mind kept reverting to the events of the night before. Tia decided to get everything organized for the next day. She planned to go in with extra steam and knock out the work that she slacked on.

While updating the next day's "to do" list, Tia got a notification of a new email, from *Sean.*

CHAPTER FIVE

Ken walked into his office and decided not to waste another minute before calling his big brother. "Yo, holler at a brother," Ken said when Charles' voicemail answered giving his "away" message. Charles must have been in court because he always made it a point to get in the office early on Monday mornings. His clientele had a tendency of getting into situations over the weekend that had them begging for his services by daybreak on Monday.

Ken just wanted to remind him that Tia was one of his best friends *and* that she is married. Charles was one of those players whose motto is "every man for himself". Under normal circumstances, a honey could be married to The Pope and Charles would not give a damn, but Ken was hoping that his big brother would cut him some slack. Ken knew that Tia was Mrs. Faithful herself, but he also knew that his brother had some hypnotizing, mind- blowing shit going on that could make even the most faithful ones falter. Ken really didn't think that Charles realized this power, which is the reason for his concern; that and Ken's uncontrollable need to protect Tia.

Ken thought about the night before. Tia *was* looking good. He hadn't seen her look like that in a while and it caught him off guard because she was alone. He hadn't been in protection mode since Tia had gotten married. He laughed to himself as he realized that Tia had someone else to protect her now and that she probably never needed his protection.

It was something about the ease Tia displayed while casually talking with Charles. She was never that comfortable talking with him in the past. She would get nervous or stupid if he even said, "What's up?" to her. Ken would always try to convince Tia that Charles was cool, even though he practiced law and was seven years older than the two of them. *Maybe it was the alcohol,* Ken thought as he tried to blow his thoughts off. Alcohol is known to make a person more comfortable in his or her own skin.

Raquel had been all over Ken that night, but he was not feeling her. He tried to back her up as nicely as he could, but she was not hearing it. Ken told Raquel that her drinks were on him for the night in hopes that she would start working the room knowing that her drinks were paid for. When that didn't work, Ken joined a group of friends nearby in a conversation about the NFL draft. Raquel patiently kept Ken's spot secured while every player was critiqued. Although Raquel wanted to stay at Ken's that night, Ken was steadfast. He did stay with Raquel, but at her place, so he could get up and leave when he was ready. He wanted to be the one in control of how long the visit was going to last.

Raquel was alright, but nothing more. She was fine as hell, but her personality needed some work. She wasn't stuck-up or bitchy, she wasn't dumb or ditsy, but she didn't have anything exciting going on either. She didn't even know how to work that sexy ass body she had. She would just serve it up at any time any way Ken wanted it. Ken never knew if she wanted him, just that she was available when he wanted her.

Ken had been thinking long-term and Raquel was nowhere in his thoughts. In fact, none of the women that he was involved with appeared in his long-term fantasies. Ken wanted to be in a serious relationship, but he did have his hang-ups. He wanted his woman fine. He wanted his woman smart. He wanted his woman to be ambitious and to know how to make him feel like a king. He wanted sexy, caring, and attentive, but behind all of that, he wanted someone who would crack up laughing at his jokes. He wanted someone who could cook (of course). He wanted someone who could acclimate to any situation (even his sister, her four children and three "baby-daddies). In the weeding process, Ken's inventory was getting low, and he didn't even care. He was secretly tired of running the streets with different women.

"See you tomorrow, I'm outta here," Tia said bringing Ken back to reality.

Ken looked at his watch, mockingly. He was surprised because it was unlike Tia to leave early. She was normally one of the last to leave. "That's what you get for trying to hang with the big dogs, T. I thought you knew that. Go home, catch up on your rest, and don't ever bust up on my set again unless you have the next day off", Ken said with that silly smirk on his face that said; listen to your big brother if you know what's good for you.

"Boy, please! The only reason I am a little out of sorts today is because it was just *too much sweat last night*," Tia said dramatically. "It started before I even made it to your spot if you really want to know. And Charles was the bonus. I couldn't believe it when I realized who he was, but I had to play it. Did I pull it off? He always treats me like a little girl."

Ken sat at his large oak desk and looked at Tia and smiled. He hadn't seen her that animated in years, and it was cute. *She had to 'play it'*, Ken thought to himself. He decided not to let her know that she 'played it' like a pro. He felt relieved to know that Tia's ease the night before was fake.

"Tia, you're his *little* brother's *little* friend, remember? And your boy would have told you who all was going to be there, *but* oh, your boy didn't even know that you were coming." Ken added his sarcasm.

"Oh, I wonder if *my boy* was going to tell me that Raquel was going to be there, or if *my boy* was going to continue to have me think that Raquel was history and that he was moving on to bigger and better things." Tia shot sarcasm right back at him.

Touché. Tia was Ken's girl, and she knew how to get him. Tia knew, from her own observations, that Ken wanted something deeper. He would never admit it to anyone else, but Tia had him pegged and had read between all the lines, correctly.

"Yo man, Raquel *is* history", Ken said, "she just doesn't know it yet."

They both laughed. Ken stood and walked around his desk; he was going to walk Tia out. Tia walked further into Ken's office; she was going to slug him one for being a jerk. When they met at the front of Ken's desk, he put an arm around her neck (purposely adding extra weight to it). "Man, it was good seeing you out there like that. Next time let a brotha know and we can do it like old times," Ken said with honesty.

"That was a spur of the moment thing last night, but something is telling me I will be there again. I may let you hang with me next time," Tia joked and winked at her friend.

Ken's arm was still resting on Tia's neck when he told her he would walk her out. Ken thought that some small talk might give him some insight as to what her and Charles had talked about for so long.

Tia seemed to be much more carefree than normal. Everything was so funny to her. She had noticed every woman that had approached Ken the night before and questioned him about each encounter. Ken told Tia what she wanted to know about the night before because he wanted some information of his own. He was used to sharing the intimate details of his life with Tia, although he hadn't done so in a while; since Tia got married and they stopped hanging out like that.

Tia told Ken that she was pleasantly surprised to see Lacey and that she didn't know she hung out there. He was surprised as well, and Ken explained that it was the first time that he had run into Lacey at Christopher's and assured Tia that it had not been planned. Tia told her friend that she thought the girl wearing the blue jersey dress was the cutest of the bunch. "Morgan. Yeah, she's straight," Ken agreed. "My boy's sister, though. So, I am trying to hold her off until I get my shit together, you know? I don't want to have to hurt her brother", Ken said with a faked arrogance.

"When did *you* get a conscience?" Tia asked. "I must really be out of touch," she said as they got to the lobby.

"Probably around the same time you got a husband," Ken shot back as he stopped. "I'll see you tomorrow. Make sure you get some rest."

"Byyyeee, Ken." Tia sang.

CHAPTER SIX

Tia had seen Sean a couple of times since they met two weeks ago, but they talked every day. Sometimes they talked for hours at a time. She noticed that she was spending a lot of time thinking about the conversations that they had. She thought about future conversations. She prepared things to talk about with him. She was fascinated by Sean's confident attitude. She loved the way he seemed so sure about everything that he did.

Sean had asked Tia to dinner a couple of days after they met. Although Tia wanted to go, she couldn't figure out a way to get away from her daily routine, so she canceled thirty minutes before she was supposed to meet him. The next day Sean asked Tia to lunch because he sensed she had a problem getting out in the evenings. Again, Tia wanted to meet him, but didn't feel comfortable going to lunch with a man that had sparked her excitement. She just didn't show.

Tia sat at her desk, dazed. She could not believe that she had stood Sean up. That used to be a regular thing for Tia when she was single. She would agree to go out with someone, but if something else came up she would just not show. She left it up to the men to decide whether they ever wanted to see her again or not. However, she felt very juvenile doing this to Sean.

It wasn't intentional and it wasn't like it was in the past. The reason that Tia was not sitting in a restaurant, having lunch with her new friend, was nerves. When she said yes to Sean the day before, she meant it. She barely slept a wink that night. She had gone to work ready the next day. She wore a nice, fitted pantsuit with a crisp white shirt and the YSL pumps that Ken and Carl commented on every time they saw her in them. Her plan was to look as if the lunch could have been a business meeting.

When twelve o'clock came, Tia started to feel like she didn't want to go. But she wanted to see Sean, so she went to touch up her face to be ready to leave the office by twelve thirty. When Tia returned from the ladies' room she sat at her desk and decided not to go. She thought about the lengthy conversations that she had had with Sean. They had not been sexual or inappropriate at all, but they were intimate. Tia had told Sean things that she had never even told her best friend, Zena; things that she would probably never tell Carl. She had never told *anyone* about her father and the fact that she didn't even know what his name was, but she told Sean. The kicker was that he did not have the least bit of shock or surprise in his voice when he replied, "Have you ever tried to find him? It wouldn't be that hard to do." She didn't know if she was embarrassed for opening up to Sean so quickly or what the problem was. All she knew was that she could not face him today.

Her cell phone rang, and she jumped. It was 1:15 and she should have been there at 1:00. She didn't know whether to answer the phone or not, so she didn't. Tia felt like she had a rock in the pit of her stomach. *What am I doing?* Tia was thinking when she heard the message indicator from her cell phone. She checked the message and felt even worse when she heard Sean's voice. "Hey. Where are you? I hope you didn't chicken out on me. Let me know something because I am starving. Alright, baby? Talk to you soon."

OMG! OMG! OMG! Tia thought, *how can I stand him up? All I have to do is call him and let him know that I won't be there so he can do his thing.* But she didn't. She sat at her desk, nervous and confused for the rest of the afternoon.

Tia walked past Ken's office on her way out and realized that she hadn't heard much from him all day. She said "bye" and Ken replied "a'ight". Tia knew that Ken must be up to something important to keep him quiet for the entire day.

She drove home and tried to get her head clear. She felt a bit of relief that she had gotten rid of Sean, but Tia wished that she had handled it better. Now he would see her as silly and immature.

Carlton and Tianna ran to the car to greet their mother when they heard the garage door close. "Mommy, Mommy we're going to Grandma's", they screamed in unison. "Do you want to come with us?" Tianna asked.

"I don't think so, honey." Tia said. "Let me talk to your dad to find out what's going on."

"Hi, Hon." Carl greeted Tia with a kiss. "I was going to go by Mom's for a while. She made her stew so don't worry about cooking. We'll bring you some."

"Oh", was Tia's reply. "Don't you want me to go?"

"Yeah right, T", said Carl. "You already know that I want you to go. I just know how you are, and I know that you probably don't want to go sit at my mother's house unless there is a special reason for being there."

Tia smiled. She appreciated her husband's understanding attitude. She liked Carl's mother, but it was the mother-in-law daughter-in-law constant competition thing that she didn't like. Tia used to go out of her way to appease Althea. These days it was easier to avoid her altogether.

Carl knew that his mother was crazy about him, and he knew just how overbearing she could be. He also knew that Tia was nothing nice once someone became an official enemy. The two of them were at least tolerant of each other so far. So, Carl tried not to force the situation unnecessarily.

"It's a good thing that I'm tired because you guys have plans of your own that don't include Mommy, huh." Tia chided. "Tell Grandma that I said 'hi' and give her a kiss for me." Tia winked at Carl.

Carl kissed his wife again, strapped the kids in and pulled off. He was glad to get out of there without Tia. He knew that his brother, Craig, would be over his mother's and they needed to talk.

CHAPTER SEVEN

Carl and Craig put together some software for police officers to get complete driving records more quickly and efficiently. They had worked on it for years. Craig being a captain on the police force and Carl being a computer (geek) programmer, they had a wealth of knowledge on what was needed and how to make it happen.

Craig had hooked it up so that the system was tested by the local agency that he worked for and that led to a two-year contract with the state agency. The idea had gotten rave reviews because of its ability to check the complete history of the vehicle being stopped, and the criminal and driving records of the registered owner of the vehicle within seconds of voice activation. Driver's licenses from any state within the United States could also be scanned and complete records pulled instantly.

The two were one year into their contract with the state when they received an offer from a computer company to buy the system. Carl was ready to sign it over as soon as he received the offer a couple of weeks ago. However, Craig thought it would be more beneficial financially to continue to contract the system out, but to go nationwide.

Carl was more than happy with the profit he made from the two-year lease, but Craig felt that they could continue to add to the system and continue to upgrade it and continue to increase the value on it. Carl wanted to go over some details with his brother to make the right decision for them both.

Carl had not mentioned the offer to Tia, which is why he didn't want her around when he spoke to Craig. He hadn't told their mother either, so he hoped that Craig had not said anything. This was a project that the two of them worked on while just hanging out together on weekends; it was something that they both had fun doing. Carl did not want any of the women in their lives to get involved and make it messy, so he would try to keep them out of it for as long as possible. He wanted to surprise them both.

Carl pulled into his mother's driveway to find his brother's Ford F150 already there. He took the children out of the car and went into his mother's house. Carl loved the way his mother's house always smelled of something good to eat. She came walking out of the kitchen with open arms when she heard the door close.

"Grandma, Grandma", the children both ran into her open arms.

"Ooooooh, Grandma misses her babies." she said squeezing them both before she went over to give Carl a kiss on the cheek.

"Hi, Ma. Where's Craig?" Carl asked as he walked towards the kitchen.

"You know where he is. Why would you even ask?" Althea said, walking behind her son.

The two of them reached the kitchen to find Craig running around the island with his niece and nephew chasing him. "We're gonna beat Uncle Craig up, Dad, because he

26

hasn't come to see us in a long time." Tianna said smiling up at her father and grandmother.

"He hasn't?" Althea said. "You *should* beat him. He's a bad uncle."

"Man, could you get your Bay Bays?" Craig begged while trying to protect himself.

"Guys, come on we'll get him for that one later." Carl said. "Grandma is making our plates right now and I think her stew is more important than Uncle Craig's beatdown."

The three adults laughed while Carl literally pulled Carlton and Tianna off their uncle. "You better go and see my babies." Althea scolded her son while she gave them all everything they needed. She loved waiting on her family. She didn't see any of them nearly as much as she wanted to. They all talked and laughed throughout the meal. When they were done, Althea cleaned the table and started to wash the dishes. When she finished, her two sons went into the den, and she had her grandchildren all to herself.

CHAPTER EIGHT

S ean called the waiter over and placed his order at 1:15. When Tia didn't answer his call, everything in him told him that she wouldn't be there. He was starving. He ate at 1:00 every day. If she had answered, he would have waited all day if he had to. Now if he waited and she didn't show, the disappointment would have been too much. He would have tortured himself with the shoulda, woulda, coulda syndrome. As he waited for his order, Sean wondered why Tia did not come. He knew that there was a chance that she would walk through the door at any second but didn't want to dwell on that.

Sean could not understand why he wanted to see Tia so badly. He kept waking with thoughts of her in his head. When she accepted his lunch offer, he actually thought about what he should wear. Sean normally dressed casually during the day unless he had to meet with someone important. He wondered how Tia dressed for work because she seemed to work in a casual environment, he didn't want to make her uncomfortable. He decided on khakis and a button down shirt which he considered middle of the road. They were meeting downtown and if one of Tia's colleagues happened to see her it could have passed for a power lunch. *What a waste,* Sean thought to himself as the food arrived. He could not recall *ever* choosing an outfit because of a woman.

Sean ate the crab cakes and chicken Caesar salad that the waiter had given him while he continued to ponder about Tia. He thought of all the reasons why she *may* not have come, but he *knew* the real reason. Sean wanted to see Tia and he knew the feelings were mutual. His conversation with her was so relaxed and comfortable that Sean felt like he had known Tia for years. It seemed only natural to want to be in her presence. Sean thought that Tia had to feel it too.

Sean decided not to beat himself up about a situation that he did not have full control of. He had gotten stood up for the first time in years and that was grounds for dismissal. *My time is much too valuable for this,* he thought, as he considered all the things that he could, no *should* have been doing that afternoon.

Sean's demeanor was strictly business, highly organized, and he never had a problem prioritizing. Although he worked for himself, Sean kept firm hours and restricted himself to no more than 1-hour lunch breaks unless it was business related. After work it was time for his children and family; they did homework, dinner and daily talks. Gina, Sean's wife, didn't have a time slot in the schedule because she didn't require much. Therefore, he had evenings to do what *he* wanted to do. Usually, he would try to check out a new movie, hang out with some of the boys and shoot pool or just check out some local hotspots. A lot of evenings were spent researching projects that could really be classified as work, but Sean enjoyed it. However, he spent the last couple of evenings on the phone with Tia, trying to figure out how he could see her again.

Sean paid his bill and left the restaurant feeling a little bad that he had driven out of his way for nothing. He had passed quite a few nice restaurants to get to the one where he was to meet Tia, and she didn't even show up. The thing that bothered him most was that he was not even mad; disappointed, but not mad. What was he thinking? *Time is money,* he told himself and he knew that he had none to waste, of either.

He drove himself back to the office and had a productive afternoon. He had tons of messages and emails waiting for him. That is just what Sean wanted, and needed, to curb his distraction.

CHAPTER NINE

Tia was thankful for some time alone. She could not remember the last time she had been at home alone. She got undressed and laid in bed in her camisole and lace thong. Tia thought about meditating because she wanted to calm her state of mind, but her next thought was of Sean. She wondered what he thought of her; probably that she was irresponsible with no respect for time. She knew that he had written her off, so she tried to tell herself that it didn't matter what he thought of her. That's when she decided that she wanted to make sure that Sean did not mistake her for being a thoughtless and inconsiderate person.

Tia got up, grabbed her laptop and began typing an email to send to Sean apologizing for wasting his time.

Hi Sean,

I'm sorry that I didn't make it today and I don't want to waste anymore of your time. I have a lot going on right now, so it's not a good time for me to try to incorporate a new friend in my life. I hope there are no hard feelings.

Best wishes,

Tia

Tia read the words that she had written over and over. Even though she revised the few words at least five times, she wondered if it sounded sincere. She wondered if it was direct enough, was it clear enough. She wondered what Sean would think when he read it. Tia wondered why she could not put together a simple 3-sentence email and make it sound the way she felt when she had been writing her whole life; she had written short stories, essays and published articles. Tia read the email once again.

Tia thought about adding something to it, then she thought about making it even shorter by just apologizing. She decided against it when she remembered that she gets paid to write other people's thoughts and ideas *and* had been successful at it for years. She assured herself that the email was perfect and pressed send.

Tia sat looking at her computer wondering if she had done the right thing when she began to feel some relief. Could Sean have been on her mind that heavily that it had caused her stress? She felt better, but she couldn't understand why. She decided that she felt better because she was not 100% sure that the brief friendship had been innocent. Although nothing had happened, Tia enjoyed talking to Sean. Now she did not have to make any decisions concerning him. *It's a done deal,* Tia thought to herself. She went to shut down her computer when she heard the email alert.

Tia almost jumped out of her thong when the soft chime sounded. It was Sean! Had he been sitting in front of the computer? Tia had never considered that. She never even thought that he would respond. Her heart pounded as she double clicked his name.

Hi Tia,

Your apology is accepted. I realize that you are a busy lady. That is why I have prepared myself for an interesting game of Cat and Mouse. I'm sure that we both know who the mouse is. Your new friend, Sean

Tia's mouth was on the floor. She could not believe what she read and reread and reread. She had so many thoughts in her head that Tia felt dizzy.

The first time she read the email she realized that she was smiling to herself. After reading it maybe three times, Tia got offended. *I am ending this thing (whatever it is),* she thought. *How dare he say "no". Is that what he said?* Tia questioned herself. A *game* of Cat and Mouse.

Tia thought about Sean's words. *Did he think I was playing a game,* Tia thought, *or was he playing?* Tia became furious. *And, no, I don't know who the mouse is,* she thought. *All I know is that it is not me because I am not timid, and Tia Lawson does not run away. This guy does not know who he is dealing with,* Tia thought. *The nerve!*

She did not reply because she could not come up with an appropriate response for Sean's email. She didn't want to respond while she was pissed off because she had a feeling he would be able to pick up on it just as she had picked up on the sarcasm in Sean's email.

The other reason that Tia did not respond to Sean's email is because she remembered that she had a class tomorrow, and she had an assignment that was due. Tia had started the master's program only a couple of months ago. It wasn't that she needed her master's for any particular reason. It was the fact that Tia had been bored and she felt like she had been transformed into just Mommy or wifey. She did not want to think of herself that way, so she decided to always make sure she did something that was only for her. Having her master's couldn't hurt her life in anyway, but she needed to get on the ball if she really wanted to do this.

CHAPTER TEN

Sean could not believe the email that Tia had sent him. This woman was a trip. Did she really think that she was going to leave him hanging and dismiss him too? He had convinced himself not to call her because of the way she dissed him, but the email got him a little hot under the collar; he had to reply.

Sean sat in his home office and tried to get back to what he was doing before he received Tia's email, but it was too late. He was distracted. So, he just waited for the reply that he was sure Tia would send. He waited and waited. Before he knew it, thirty minutes had gone by. He had not done anything but think about Tia. She didn't come off as the game playing type, that's why her little email surprised him.

Still, there was no reply. He had to call her.

Sean dialed Tia's number, but had no idea what he was going to say. She answered on the first ring. "Woman, I refuse to let you stand me up *and* kick me to the curb all in one day and I haven't even taken you out yet." Sean said nervously, hoping that he was saying the right thing.

"What?" Tia couldn't help smiling.

Sean was relieved to hear Tia's smile through the phone line.

"Your Dear John letter… I'm not havin' it." Sean said with more ease. "I can't believe that you would leave me in a restaurant alone, staring at the door all afternoon and then top that with leave me alone I'm too busy for you."

"Oh, is that what you read?" Tia said, still smiling.

"Yes, I read what you wrote."

"No, I don't think that's quite what I wrote."

"The active word in that sentence was *quite*." Sean said sarcastically. "Well, I have it right here if you need me to read it to you. That way you may get a better understanding of what I really said." Tia jumped at an opportunity to explain herself.

"Only if it's done in person." Sean was gaining confidence.

Silence.

"Hello?" Sean hoped she hadn't hung up on him.

"I'm here." Other than those two words, Tia was speechless.

"Is it a problem, Tia?"

"Not at all." Tia regained her composure. "When?"

"As soon as possible; tomorrow." Sean was hopeful.

"That's fine."

"I won't hold my breath because I'm not ready to die."

"I wouldn't let you die." Tia said as she heard the garage door open.

"I'll call you in the morning for the details, okay?" Tia tried not to sound rushed.

"Okay, but do you have to go?"

"You said you realized that I'm a busy lady."

"And the perfect little mouse. I'll be waiting for your call."

"Goodnight." Tia was smiling. She didn't want the call to end. "Moooommy" Carlton whined before opening Tia's bedroom door.

Before Sean could say goodnight, the phone was dead, and he felt a strange emptiness inside.

CHAPTER ELEVEN

Carlton and Tianna walked into the bedroom before Carl.
They both ran and jumped on the bed with Tia as she
hurried to shut down her laptop. They both smelled fresh,
and they were wearing pajamas that Tia had never seen
before.

"Well don't you two smell good." Tia said as she took a
big whiff of her two beautiful children.

"Grandma gave us a bath and she gave us these new pjs
too." Tianna exclaimed.

"Well, that was very nice of Grandma."

Tia held Carlton and Tianna on top of her as she lied in
bed and felt totally peaceful.

Carl entered their bedroom and kissed Tia on the lips.
Both children looked at their parents and made faces as if they
were grossed out. Carl and Tia laughed. They both loved their
children. That was undeniable.

"Mom wanted to bathe them for you. She had bought
them pajamas in case they spent the night unexpectedly. She
said they should bring them home before they grow out of
them."

"That was very nice of her. I will have to give her a call
to thank her."

"Your food is in the kitchen. Would you like me to heat it for you?"

"No thanks, Honey. I don't want to eat so late. I'm going to read a story with Tianna and Carlton before I put them to bed. Why don't you go ahead and shower while I take care of them?"

Normally Tia would read the beginning of the story to set the pace. Then Tianna and Carlton would each read a page or two and Tia would finish. Tonight, both children were fast asleep by the time Tia finished reading the first three pages of the book. Tia wondered what they did at their grandmother's house that had them so tired.

Tia thought about the next day and what she would wear as she walked back into her bedroom. She walked into her closet and began to think about how she wanted to look when she saw Sean. She was startled when she heard Carl turn on the water for the shower. She thought he had showered while she was with the children.

Tia decided to jump in the shower with Carl. They used to shower together almost every evening. It seemed to be a good time for them to catch up on family and household issues. They would discuss events of the day and have general conversation in the intimate setting of their large marble shower.

Tia walked into the bathroom and saw her husband's silhouette through the steamed glass shower doors. He obviously did not hear her come in and he continued to twist and turn his long lean body under the hot water. Carl had all three shower heads on full blast, and he seemed to be enjoying the relief that the pounding hot water brought. Tia was enjoying watching the water drip off her husband's body. The room was filled with steam and the fragrance of the

Cartier body wash that Carl used. Carl turned and bent his neck down so that the water would hit him in the perfect spot. Carl moaned. The sound turned Tia on, and she moaned herself without realizing it.

Carl looked up and was surprised to see Tia standing there staring at him. "Hey, you coming?"

Tia smirked and answered by letting her silk, chocolate brown robe drop to the floor. She opened one of the shower doors and stepped inside. Carl tried to move so that Tia could get to the spot that she liked in the shower, but he stopped when he felt the palm of Tia's hand on his pelvic bone pushing him against the wall.

Tia was wet before she put one foot into the shower. As soon as the shower door was closed, she wanted to devour Carl. She pushed him into the wall so that he could support himself while she tasted the head of his limp dick. Tia liked the smoothness of the tip of Carl's muscle, and she ran her tongue around it again and again until she felt the shaft throbbing in the palm of her hand. Her tongue went from the head to the shaft in a slow methodical rhythm. She applied pressure in circular motions to Carl's balls with the palm of her hand while she tried to consume his entire manhood with her mouth over and over again. She licked the tip, then the shaft and then took him entirely into her mouth. Carl wanted to kiss Tia. He tried to bring her face up to his, but she refused. She licked the inside of Carl's thighs down to his knees and back up again, stroking him while licking the water from his body. When Tia was ready, she stood and began licking and kissing Carl's hairy chest. She licked his nipples then sucked them. She kissed and licked the length of Carl's rippled abdomen. Tia was heated.

Carl was in a daze. He wanted to control himself, but it was difficult with his wife all over him the way that she was. Carl knew that if he lost control even for a second that it would be a premature climax. He didn't want it to end that way, so he tried again to kiss his wife. This time Tia allowed him to kiss her.

Carl picked Tia up so that they were eye to eye, and he kissed her slowly and lovingly. He was secretly trying to regain his composure. He could tell that it was not going to be easy by the way that Tia wrapped her tongue around his, again and again. He raised her a little higher and he slowly licked the roundness of each breast before he let her feet touch the marble flooring again. Then Carl bent down to put his tongue into Tia's navel. He ran his tongue from the inside of her navel to the top of her forest and back before Tia grabbed his hand and began to pull Carl out of the shower.

Tia didn't want the slow, nice and easy love making that they had become accustomed to. She wanted heated passion. She didn't want to slow it down at all, so when Carl tried to lead her to the bed she said "no" and pushed him on the double sink countertop instead…she had just gotten started.

Carl leaned back while Tia resumed licking and kissing him from top to bottom. She licked him from back to front and then she climbed on top and slid down slowly onto him. Tia rode Carl like he was a stallion. They both panted, and moaned, and moaned, and panted before Tia felt the warmth of Carl's liquid enter her body. Carl started to move slower, but Tia continued to ride.

Tia moved her body from the tip of Carl's dick down to the base of his pelvic hairs, slowly, over and over again. She leaned her torso into Carl's upper body as she moved her pelvis in circular motions, and she slid up and down the length of Carl's penis. Tia felt herself coming to her climax and she lay on her husband's chest and continued to wind; her clitoris moving against Carl's skin and hair made Tia feel like she would explode. When she did, Tia collapsed on top of her husband for most of the night. She did even notice when he picked her up and put her in bed.

CHAPTER TWELVE

Sean was on his second Martini and beginning to feel the effects when Tia walked in. The sight of her brought him to complete sobriety. She was more eye-catching than Sean remembered. *Maybe that isn't her,* he thought because she didn't walk directly over to him.

Tia was impressed when she walked into the swanky Martini bar where she was supposed to meet Sean. He suggested that they meet there to talk because it was in a central location. Tia had never been here before, but she purposely walked in and walked over to the bar as if she were a frequent customer. She hated when she felt like she looked lost.

When she reached the bar, Tia realized that Sean was standing on the opposite end. She walked over, nervously, and brushed his cheek with her lips.

"How are you?" Tia said quickly as her lips passed Sean's ear.

Sean hoped that his lips would move. He could not believe it was Tia. When she walked to the other side of the bar, he assumed that it wasn't her. He had automatically refocused his eyes on the door and continued to wait when he felt Tia enter his personal space.

She caught him off guard with the light kiss on the cheek. When she pulled away to speak, Sean noticed how bright and pretty Tia's smile was. She was looking at him, waiting for an answer and Sean was busy trying to soak up every visual detail about Tia.

"I'm much better now." Sean finally spoke. "I thought that I was going to have to spend the evening watching the door. You look beautiful." Sean was smiling. He felt like he had run into a long-lost friend.

Tia was wearing a dress that she had picked up from Neiman Marcus a couple of months ago. It had been hanging in her closet because Tia hadn't gone anywhere to wear it. Although it was nothing fancy, it was nice and had a very feminine quality to it. Tia remembered when she bought the dress, she thought that she would wear it with Carl on one of their Sunday afternoon outings.

"I'm *only* five minutes late, but I do apologize. Customarily it's at least fifteen, but I changed that today just for you." Tia smiled and ignored Sean's comment about how she looked.

She planned to look nice, but casual; not like she had gotten dressed just for him. She also *needed* to look casual to get out of the house with Carl thinking that she was on her way to class. She decided to ditch her class for the night since she didn't have the time or the focus to complete her assignment. Tia also thought it would be the perfect time to get her meeting with Sean behind her.

Tia and Sean sat and talked, and laughed, and drank martinis for hours before either of them noticed the time. Sean looked down at his Rolex and was shocked. He had made dinner reservations for an hour ago. He didn't know if

Tia wanted to have dinner or not, but he made the reservation to be safe.

"Would you like to get something to eat? I'm hungry." Sean felt the anxiety after he spoke. He hoped that Tia would join him for dinner. Although they missed the reservation at the Ocean Grill, Sean knew that he would be able to get a table, even if he had to slip something to the Maître D.

"Yes, I think I need to eat something." Tia felt the effects of the alcohol on her brain and her body. "I don't want to pass out on you."

Sean motioned for the waiter so that he could take care of the bill and the two of them walked out.

Tia and Sean enjoyed an interesting conversation over dinner. Although the topics were general, you know, children, life goals, career paths, parents, and belief and or disbelief in true, life-lasting love. It seemed very intimate to Tia. She shared some things over that dinner that she had never shared with anyone and had never planned to.

When Sean asked about Tia's father again, Tia's reply was "I have tried to look for him to no avail. It seems to be very painful for my mother, so I don't even ask her anymore." Ever since Tia could remember, she had looked for a good (appropriate) answer for the father question. Never had she considered the truth, so she wondered where it had come from.

Sean told Tia how his father had left his mother with three small children and one still growing in his mother's belly. He told her how that situation affected his relationship with his own children and about his current relationship with his father.

Tia was startled by the way she felt. While Sean spoke, Tia felt like some dreamy eyed teenager out on a date with

Jay-Z or some shit. She kept reminding herself to stay cool and that she had heard it all before (in some form). She was not sure that she would be able to pull it off.

The conversation began to lean towards business and work. Tia could not explain why she felt unsure of herself. She did not have any idea why she did not want to talk extensively about her job, and she did not ask many questions about his business. She did not understand why at that moment she felt plain dumb; and Tia had always been at the top of her class, always knowledgeable about finance and current events and always confident about who she was. She did not know if her feelings were caused by the way Sean spoke about his business endeavors or by the super confident way Sean talked about real estate, the market and the financial state that the country was in. All Tia knew is that she wanted to shake the feeling and snap back to the person she really was.

Tia realized that, if nothing else, her uncertainties had removed her from the trancelike state that she had been in. *Maybe it's the alcohol,* Tia thought. She remembered that she did not *normally* drink as much as she had tonight. Tia was comfortable placing the blame on the drinks. *That's all it was,* she thought, to convince herself even more.

Sean noticed that Tia seemed worried about something. He hoped that she did not regret having dinner with him. He had really enjoyed her company. He knew that they should be leaving, but he didn't want to. Sean reached across the table and grabbed Tia's hand, before he could even think better about what he was doing. "Is everything alright?" Sean asked Tia.

"Yeah. Yeah, I'm okay." Tia replied quickly with a light smile. "What time is it?"

"It's late. I guess we should be going", Sean replied. He didn't want to tell her the exact time because he didn't want to upset her. It was 1:00 AM.

The conversation lightened while Sean and Tia waited to pay the bill.

CHAPTER THIRTEEN

Tia could not concentrate at work. She could not believe what she had done.

Carl was fast asleep when Tia walked into their bedroom still slightly mesmerized by her evening. She was a little surprised that Carl did not so much as stir. She was also surprised that she didn't feel the slightest bit of guilt as she looked over at her husband sleeping peacefully.

That morning Tia explained to Carl how some of the students in the class, including herself, decided to form a study group, first meeting immediately after class. She excitedly told him how they all talked for a couple hours then decided to go out for drinks while Carl read the newspaper. No questions asked.

Tia's mind was on Sean; 100%. If she were not working for her boy, Tia probably would have called out for the day. Her mind was definitely out. Ken wouldn't be in until later, but Tia wanted to make sure that everything was in order when he did get in the office, so she really needed to get it together quickly.

Tia decided to throw on some music to wake herself up. She browsed through her music file and decided that Jill Scott would bring her back to consciousness as she checked her selection. Music was always a mood enhancer for Tia. She listened to the Neo-Soul sound as she responded to Ken's email that needed urgent attention and wondered what it was about Sean that intrigued her.

Ken burst into the office at about 11:30, laptop on his shoulder but looking quite leisurely. What surprised Tia was what Ken was wearing. Although they didn't have an official dress code, everyone kept it professional. And Ken maintained that standard today even though he was wearing jeans. He wore a Robert Graham shirt, which hung perfectly, with black Gucci loafers. The haircut was tight. Ken smelled yummy and looked even better.

"What's up?" Tia asked realizing that she had not even asked Ken why he would be late. She didn't think that he had anything scheduled for the morning but he looked like he could have been handling some business. Tia had just finished preparing everything Ken needed for the meeting tomorrow.

"Hey, hey", was Ken's reply as he breezed by Tia's office and went straight into his.

"Uh?" Tia made a mental note to get in Ken's business later. She had a feeling something was awry. Ken would normally make sure that Tia knew all his comings and goings, so if anything important came up she would know how to get to him and/or how to cover for him. Today, however, Tia had come into the office to find only a voicemail from her boss saying that he would be in late. She knew Ken well enough to know that he purposely avoided speaking to her. Otherwise, he would have called her on her cell phone.

Tia jumped to get her purse at the thought of her cell phone. She had not even taken it out of her purse, and she knew that she could not hear the phone if it rung. When she got to her phone, she saw that she had two voice messages.

Tia did not look at the call log to see who had called but went straight to voicemail.

"Good morning, Tia, I hope I didn't call too early. I should have told you to call me to let me know that you made it home safely. I didn't, so now I'm here beating myself up about it. Call me."

The last one was a hang up.

CHAPTER FOURTEEN

Sean sat in his office and thought about Tia. He thought about the night before in disbelief. He could not believe that he couldn't get Tia off his mind. He could barely get to sleep last night because he was thinking about her. He knew that she had a couple of Martinis and wondered if she would be able to drive home safely. He wanted to tell her to call him when she made it home but didn't because he did not want Tia to think that he was being pushy. Sean really wanted to talk to Tia while she drove home but thought she would have called him if she felt the same.

He called Tia as soon as he finished his morning workout. She didn't answer and he left a message. His reasoning for the early morning call was that he wanted to make sure she had gotten home safely. It was already after noon and Tia had not returned his call. Now Sean was genuinely concerned. He wondered if she had a problem at home for coming in so late. He didn't know if she was avoiding him, although she didn't seem to be the type. He tried to block the thought that something may have happened on her way home last night.

He called again. Voicemail.

"Hey, Tia. I hate to call you like this, but I was kind of tipsy last night. I know that you were too, so I just want to clear my conscience and find out if you are safe and sound."

Sean rationalized his apparent concern by reminding himself that they just met, and he did not know her drinking capacity.

Sean questioned this attraction to Tia. He needed to know what was driving it.

He thought about his wife and all the time they had been together. He loved Gina, but things had changed between them. She never really snapped back after her mother died. He had not been interested in another woman in years, though. Sean saw women, talked to women, did business with women and even entertained them from time to time but he had never gotten distracted this way before. He didn't even know why he had stopped to talk to Tia the night they met, but he did know that he liked her from the first conversation.

He had to get himself together. Sean had rescheduled a 10:00 meeting to 1:00 because he wanted to be available when Tia called. It was almost 1:00 and Sean was aggravated, partly because he had not heard anything from Tia, nor had he gotten anything done. He needed to be sharp for the meeting with this attorney and Sean just did not feel up to decoding the legal jargon right now.

Sean was not one to beat around the bush or play the game, so he tried calling Tia again. No answer.

"Hey again, Tia. Just a little concerned that I haven't heard from you. I hope everything is alright". Sean felt uneasy. He was honestly just troubled because he couldn't contact Tia, but why?

Sean was distracted throughout most of the meeting, but he felt good because things were going in his favor. His lawyer, Jeremy, was negotiating a contract with a difficult client. Sean thought that they would have to revise the contract but was surprised that Jeremy had gotten him to agree to most of the terms. The client only needed Sean to give him more time; a couple more weeks Jeremy said. Sean told Jeremy that he would allow no more than 10 business days, although he was a month ahead of schedule.

Sean and Jeremy discussed their business before they put each other up on what they knew about the local happenings. The Eatery was packed and Jeremy knew quite a few of the customers that walked in because his office was in the same building. The women made sure to stop by the table to say their "hellos".

Overall, the meeting took Sean's mind off Tia. He thought about the way Jeremy juggled women and smiled. He had been Sean's attorney for years and they had grown to be friends. Jeremy was two years out of a nasty divorce, and he was just beginning to enjoy the benefits of being single. Although he didn't seem bitter about his ex making out with the house, the car, the kids and half the money that he worked for, Jeremy didn't look like he was interested in being married again any time soon.

Sean jumped a little as he remembered that he hadn't turned his cell phone ringer back on. He hadn't checked his messages or even looked at his phone since he walked in the restaurant. The Eatery was one place that enforced the "No Cell Phone" rule which was why Sean didn't usually go there during business hours. He had 5 voicemail messages and immediately checked to see who had called. There were three calls from his office, one from his sister and one call from Tia. Sean's eyes went directly to the time of Tia's call, 1:24. *That was a couple hours ago,* Sean thought as he decided to check his messages before calling her back. He dialed his voicemail and hoped he would talk to Tia soon.

Olivia's first message was that Christian's school secretary called the office for Sean and his heart was pounding hard as he listened to the next message. It was Olivia, his assistant again, she apologized for the previous message. She said she didn't want to alarm him, and Christian's teacher just wanted to schedule a conference. He felt a little better as he went to the next message. It was his sister, Karen, sounding happy as ever. She said she was just calling to say "hi" to her "little brother" because she hadn't heard from him in a while. Refreshing. Olivia called to tell him that Karen called. Didn't she know that his sister would call him on his cell? *Finally, Tia's message,* Sean thought.

"Hi, Sean, it's Tia. Yes, I made it home safely. Thank you for being concerned. Give me a call when you have time."

CHAPTER FIFTEEN

Ken hoped that Tia hadn't heard any part of what he was on the phone saying when she walked in his office. He was so engrossed in the conversation that he was having that he didn't hear her coming. Ken tried to be charming although she caught him off guard. He did the little bang bang thing with his fingers at her because she noticed that she startled him. Tia could feel the vibe and left the office quickly; she could tell that he was in the middle of something.

Ken had been on the phone with his accountant since he walked into his office. Jake was a white boy that Ken met through Charles. Charles used Jake's services also. He went to law school with Jake's older brother, so he hired him as soon as he got certified out of friendship. Jake ended up being one hell of an accountant, though. He learned all the tricks of the trade and he could find a loophole where no one else could.

Ken had the feeling that every area of his life was about to change, and he wanted to make sure that he covered his ass. Jake was Ken's accountant and Ken found out years ago that a good accountant, like a good attorney, becomes your biggest confidant, so he hired him, out of friendship, as soon as he was certified. Ken liked Jake's thinking, so he didn't mind confiding in him. In fact, he would bounce ideas off Jake from time to time that weren't even related to their business together. The fact that Jake wasn't in Ken's circle of family and/or friends really made it much easier for Ken to be honest and to trust that Jake wasn't giving a biased opinion or answer.

Today was the most emotional and honest that Ken had ever been with anyone. Jake listened without interruption for about an hour before

Tia walked in the office. Ken paused because he didn't want Tia to pick up on anything and Jake said calmly, "Dude, meet at Cheesecake in an hour. I'm buying you lunch."

Ken had a pile of work that he needed to catch up on, but he knew that he couldn't say no. Besides, he wanted to hear what Jake thought about the situation he was in. Financially, Ken knew that everything would be fine. However, the news that he got last night was going to impact much more than his finances.

Ken tried to wrap some things up at work before he left to meet Jake. He did get through a couple of important phone calls without any distractions. Ken knew that Tia would ask questions if he left without an explanation since he had already taken the morning off. He decided to go to her office to get up to speed with her about work since he had a few minutes to spare.

Ken walked into Tia's office and into the smooth sounds of Pete Belasco. Ken could only see the back of Tia because she was looking out of the window. She had her arms wrapped around a file and didn't move until Ken walked up next to her to see if she was looking at something specific. When Ken craned his neck and came face to face with Tia, she pushed him back. "What, Silly?" Tia playfully asked Ken, even though she didn't want to leave the memory she was having.

"Dang, where were you?" Ken asked as he leaned back on Tia's desk. He really wanted to know too. He went to Tia feeling guilty because he thought that he had been acting suspiciously. *Wow,* Ken thought. *Something is different about Tia.* Her outfit was hot, but that wasn't unusual. He didn't think that she had done anything different to her hair. Ken didn't know what it was, but something about Tia seemed changed.

"I'm here, at my job." Tia quipped. "What's up with you, Mr. Missing in Action?" Tia wanted to divert the attention from herself.

Tia brought Ken back to his current reality, and he remembered why he had gone to her office. "Oh yeah, I just had something that I had to take care of this morning." Ken was being evasive and hoped that it would work with his homegirl. "I came to see you to find out what's going on, and if there's anything that you need to tell me or talk to me about regarding work since I wasn't available this morning. And, no, I have not had the chance to go over the briefing for the meeting, but I will."

"Well," Tia said slowly, "I don't think there's anything that I need to speak with you about, *regarding work*. I emailed you the latest on everything." She deliberately sounded puzzled.

"I have to run out. I'm going to meet Jake over at The Cheesecake Factory. I don't know exactly how long I'm gonna be so if you need me just hit me on the cell."

"Oh-kaayy?" Tia said.

"I know, man. It's crazy. I'll tell you about it later," Ken said in confession, "but I must meet Jake in 10 minutes. You know how he's a stickler for time." Ken was about to walk out of Tia's door, and he turned and said, "You look good. You going out?"

"No, you are. Now, byyyyeeee." Tia said.

The Cheesecake Factory was five blocks away from Ken's office and he knew that it would be faster to walk than to drive. He started walking and was thankful for Tia's friendship. She knew him well and he knew her. She knew that something was up with Ken, so he felt better to address it rather than try to avoid her.

Then he thought about Raquel; she had spent the night with him just a couple of days ago. She called him when he was on his way in the shower and Ken told her that he was going to unlock his door and that he expected her to be in his bed by the time he was out of the shower.

Ken was only half surprised to find Raquel in his bed. She always did whatever he asked or told her to, but it was still hard for Ken to conceive that someone could be so controlled. He wondered sometimes if Raquel had any desires of her own. She freaked Ken just as instructed, but he found it hard to reciprocate because she didn't seem to enjoy it. Raquel was pretty cool in every area except the bedroom. Ken wished that she were more like the other women that he knew as far as "getting hers"; at least he knew that they were in on the deal. He wasn't comfortable with his relationship with Raquel because he wasn't used to having so much control over someone. He would always feel like he used her, he wondered if she felt the same. He hoped not.

Ken thought about Lacey, and he could feel the stress build up in his chest. Ken and Lacey dated consistently for about three months and Ken thought the Lacey was "the one". Suddenly, they just fell off and Ken did not know what happened. He did what he could to pull things together, but

Lacey would just call every now and again. They would go out, have a great time, make crazy love and go their separate ways. Although Ken was really into Lacey, he didn't want to seem pushy when she had already backed away from the relationship as it started to get serious.

He noticed that he was hearing from her more often within the last month but didn't read into it. Ken was a bit intimidated by Lacey because she seemed very detached. It was a little too easy for Lacey to ease off. Ken could detect a dangerous situation, so he knew to keep it cool where Lacey was concerned. He didn't want to be hurt.

She called Ken on Friday afternoon two weeks before. They went out for drinks after work, and both got wasted on Cosmos. Ken didn't wake up until the next afternoon when he could not sleep anymore because of a dreamy aroma flowing from his bathroom. Ken opened his eyes and smiled remembering the first time Lacey had showered at his house and he smelled that bath gel for the first time. He could not keep his hands off her. *Did she carry that stuff with her?* Ken thought to himself. His question was answered when Lacey sashayed in the room wearing her short, white robe. *I guess she had a plan,* Ken thought.

She went into the kitchen and came back with a tray filled with everything a man waking up from a night of alcohol could possibly want. There was fresh fruit, a bowl of soup, a turkey sandwich, a glass of ice, a bottle of water, a coke, and a kettle of hot water with a tea bag. "Wow. What time did you get up?" Ken asked as Lacey tried to reach across him to put the tray on the bed.

Ken wanted the tray and everything on it, but it could wait. He lifted his head a little to kiss her and said, "Put that over there." He pointed to the nightstand on the other side of the bed. When Lacey stood to take the tray of food to the other side, her robe opened, body glistening.

"Just put it right here." Ken said, he waited until the tray was secure and he pulled her on top of him.

They touched each other and kissed for a few minutes before Lacey took control. She drizzled his body with kisses, from head to toe and back again. Then Lacey let her tongue play slowly from Ken's chest down to his manhood, where she lost it. Lacey slowly circled the head of Ken's dick with her tongue. When she saw a droplet of clear, sticky juice on the tip of Ken's manhood, she sucked it up like it was the sweet from sugar. She circled his dickhead again with her tongue, then she went down his shaft until her mouth was full. She made sure her mouth was wet like her pussy. When she pulled back up on Ken's rock-hard dick, she allowed some of the wetness to escape so she could lick it lightly with her tongue while she stroked his balls.

Ken opened his eyes just to make sure that he wasn't dreaming. Lacey looked like she was enjoying it as much as he was; maybe more. When she looked up and their eyes met, Lacey started stroking while she was licking Ken's penis like it was a lollipop. The sight of her clearly being pleasured by pleasing him brought Ken to the ultimate climax. The sight of the cum and the taste of his volcano erupting in Lacey's mouth made Lacey cum harder than she ever had.

Before going into their self-induced coma they shared the ice water and turkey sandwich. Ken drank some of the chicken noodle soup that was now room temperature. He poured the coke into the glass that they had drunk the water from, leaned back and looked at Lacey who had already dozed off and looked so beautiful, naked and sleeping peacefully next to Ken. He remembered wishing that they could be together more often before he drifted off.

Ken woke before Lacey and jumped in the shower. He stood beneath the steaming water and thought again about having a monogamous relationship with Lacey. He enjoyed everything about her; even her aloofness was a turn-on in some twisted way. He wasn't ready for her to leave but didn't want to pressure her by asking her to stay. Ken was thinking of all the things that they could do if they spent the day together when he felt Lacey step into the shower behind him. He must have been deep in thought because he hadn't even heard her come into the bathroom.

"Do you mind?" Lacey asked before she kissed the part of his back that her lips could reach without a strain.

Ken erased the smile that tried to escape before he turned to kiss Lacey. She felt good in Ken's arms. They embraced each other under the warm water for a while before Lacey said, "you going somewhere?" and Ken would have sworn that there was uncertainty in her voice when she asked.

"I don't know. You want to?" Ken asked with his own uncertainties. He started kissing from the top of her head to her lips. He had a whole list of places they could go, but he didn't know what her plans were.

They ended up going to see a movie. They stopped at a park and talked for a while before returning to Ken's place for another night of passion.

Since then, they talked more often and seemed close again, but Ken could have never been prepared for what Lacey told him on Friday morning. When she called Ken was happy to hear from her and hoped that she wanted to get together with him.

"Is everything okay?" Ken asked because he thought he heard Lacey's voice shaking. "You sound different."

"I'm pregnant!!!" Lacey shouted through tears and snot and into the phone.

CHAPTER SIXTEEN

Lacey sat on the edge of the bed in her suburban home and shook from crying. She had cried so much that there were literally no more tears, so she sat and sobbed for what must have been hours.

Lacey cried until she made herself sick because she had to give what she thought was the worst news in the world to the only person in her life that she really loved (other than her mother). She cried because she was in no position to bring a life into the world right now. She was torn because she knew that it was now or never.

Lacey never thought that she would get pregnant because she had tried for two years with her ex-fiancé Erick. They both went through testing, and they found no medical reason why they did not conceive. The frustration of trying became too much for the relationship and they decided to break it off. Six months later Erick announced that his new girlfriend was pregnant, and they were on their way to Vegas to get married.

Since then, Lacey had forced herself to give up the idea of ever having children. She thought something was wrong with her although the doctors had assured her that it would happen. "When the time was right" she remembered people telling her. She wasn't on any type of birth control besides condoms, when necessary, and that had only been once or twice after the breakup when she thought she *had* to get on the dating scene. For the last year she had not slept with anyone besides Ken, and she quietly hoped that he wasn't sleeping around. She knew that it was a lot to expect because she didn't have anything solid or even regular with Ken. They tried but things had gotten serious really fast and unexpectedly for Lacey. She knew that Ken wanted children and a family, and she didn't want the same problems or pain that she had experienced during her engagement to Erick, so Lacey decided to back off and give Ken some space.

That, combined with the fact that she hadn't told Ken about her mother either. As far as he knew they were normal; an educated, single woman taking caring of her single mother by providing her a nice place to live. She never thought that she would have to fess up to Ken, of all people. Now there was no way to avoid it.

Before she slowed things down with Ken, Lacey tried to find a way to justify being with Ken without being able to give him a child. She thought of the many children that needed homes to be adopted into. She thought of how compassionate Ken was and knew that he would try to be understanding, but she didn't want to take that chance. Nor did she want to deprive Ken of being a father to his own son or daughter or both. She couldn't put herself out there to be rejected again.

Afterwards, when Ken started to settle into the new relationship that they had going, Lacey told herself that she had made the right decision. She would never have to tell him that she couldn't have children. They seemed as close as ever whenever they were together. The only problem came when

Ken began to complain that they weren't together enough. He would start to ask questions again about where she would go when she wasn't with him for days, sometimes weeks. He would ask to come by her house every now and then which made Lacey uncomfortable. He told her that he felt like a "bitch" because he was always waiting for her to call and give a command.

She had thought about it a thousand times, but never once imagined that she would be *forced* to tell Ken about her mother. It was an extremely sensitive subject for Lacey because it was *her mother*. It had been just the two of them since Lacey was thirteen years old when she heard the terrible things that her aunt and her grandmother said about her mother. They spoke right in front of Lacey as if they were not talking about the woman that gave birth to her.

Lacey thought her mother was the perfect mother until the day that she heard that conversation. She didn't think anything of the fact that her mother went out at night and sometimes wasn't home when Lacey left for school in the mornings. She knew that her mother drank and that her uncles would drag her into the house sometimes, but for some reason she had never thought of those things as bad or wrong until she heard *that* conversation.

Lacey remembered wondering how a mother could say such things about her very own daughter. She remembered getting so mad that she couldn't wait for her mother to come home so she could tell her the things that her own mother and sister were saying about her. When her mother came home, she was falling down drunk. Lacey told her what she heard, and that family almost tore the house down that night! Lacey had never heard so much cursing in her life. Her grandfather had the final word and said that he had better not hear another ill word spoken under his roof about any one of his children and demanded everyone in the house to join hands in prayer. Lacy still remembered her grandfather's words.

Lord we come to You in prayer today to ask for a blessing for this family, Lord. First, we want to ask You to forgive us for our sins, oh Lord. We know that each one of us here has sinned. Some of us sin in our actions, Lord. Some sin with our tongues and some of us sin in our minds, but we all have sinned and come short of Your Glory. We want Your forgiveness, Lord, we beg Your forgiveness.

My daughter has gone astray, my Lord, and we want her back. I'm asking You to wash her Lord, cleanse her, create in her a clean heart and renew a right spirit in her, Lord. Help her to cling to the people that love her, Lord, the ones that want to help her. We come to You because we know that You, and only You, can help us right now. I put my trust in You to keep this family strong. I thank You for my children, Lord and ask that You keep all my children and my family in Your loving arms of protection. We love You and we thank You in advance; in the name of Jesus, we pray. Amen.

The next morning Lacey's mother seemed different. Lacey had never seen her so serious. She told Lacey that she would not be going to school that day. Although Lacey's grandmother was in her normal spot in the kitchen cooking, the whole house seemed strange, no one was talking. Lacey wore a new outfit that her mother laid out on the bed for her, and her mother wore a pretty dress that Lacey had never seen before. Lacey and her mother ate a quiet breakfast with her grandmother and aunt Janet. All the adults at the table apologized to each other and Lacey wondered if any of them really knew the real damage that had been done. Lacey left her grandparents' house with her mother that day and they never returned.

The two of them were fine after that. Lacey didn't know what her mother did at night, but she was home when she got up for school in the mornings making breakfast. She would be at home when Lacey went to bed and things seemed normal to Lacey. It wasn't until Lacey went off to college that things started going downhill for her mother. Lacey thought it was loneliness, so as soon as she graduated and started working, she bought a house for the two of them. However, it was too late for a quick fix. Mary needed professional help. They had been in and out of programs ever since, but they were managing. Lacey knew they could do it; until this.

Her head felt like it would burst from the pressure. Although she didn't want to ruin Ken's life, she *had* to have this baby because this could be her only chance at motherhood. When she called him, it was more of reaching out to him as a friend than as the father of the child she had just found out she was carrying. She didn't know who else to call. She didn't have anyone else to call. At a time when she should have been able to, she couldn't call her mother. She didn't communicate with anyone in her family *because* of her mother. Lacey didn't get close to anyone as a friend because she always wanted to be available if or when her mother needed her, and she knew that friends could be very time consuming. The only reason that Lacey found a way to keep Ken in her life is because he was her only source of enjoyment, and she could not stand to lose him.

This was all too much. She didn't think she could have children, but she was pregnant. Ken was the father, and this would probably be the *only* unplanned event in his life. She had kept and controlled the secret about her mother for most of her life and now she would *have* to tell it. She would not be shocked if Ken vanished after he finds out that his child's grandmother is a crackhead.

CHAPTER SEVENTEEN

Sean decided to wrap up a few things at work before he tried to call Tia again. He called to schedule the conference with Christian's teacher, and then returned his sister's call. Sean missed his sister and asked her when she and the kids would be able to visit again. Karen told Sean that that was the reason for her phone call. She wanted to know what the holiday plans were and suggested that their families get together to celebrate it at either her place or his. They talked for a while and decided that they would play it by ear and decide within a week or so. The two of them had always been close and tried to visit each other as often as possible. It was uplifting for Sean, speaking and joking with Karen. He felt much better and dialed Tia as soon as he finished talking to his sister.

"Hello", Tia answered after the first ring.

"Hi, Tia. It's me, Sean. Are you busy?"

"Hey you. I was actually just thinking about calling you again. I wanted to tell you that I had a good time last night."

"That's good to hear. I enjoyed it myself. I was just concerned about you making it home safely, though."

"I wasn't really that tipsy. I'm a big girl."

"Oh, I'm pretty sure that you can handle yourself, but since you were with me, I think I would have slept better knowing that you were safe."

Tia smiled.

"So, how was your day?"

"It was good. I was a bit tired from the late night. I don't normally stay out so late; especially on weekdays."

"Does that mean that we can't do it again this evening?" Sean asked because he saw the opportunity.

"Do what?" Tia asked smiling into the phone. "Stay out late?"

"No," Sean chuckled, "have a drink, or dinner, or dinner and a drink."

Tia was quiet. She could not believe what she was hearing. All day she thought about seeing Sean again. She wanted to, but she was not expecting it to be any time soon. "No, I don't think so." Tia answered because the dead air made her uneasy.

"Okay. What do you have planned for the weekend?" Sean asked. He let the rejection roll off easily because he knew Tia's situation and he knew that it was short notice.

"I don't have any plans." Tia answered reluctantly, thinking about her normal weekends with Carl and the kids. They would go to a park, a movie, a museum or some sort of family outing every weekend unless someone was sick or something. They never planned it, but it was an unspoken thing that they did.

"You want to do something?" Sean didn't know where this was coming from but knew that if Tia agreed they would have a great time together.

"Um, I'm not sure." Tia answered and felt that little twinge that reminded her to be assertive. Sean seemed so sure

69

of himself, that she kept reminding herself to be confident when she spoke to him.

"Ok, just let me know and I'll plan something. What time do you leave work?"

"It depends. I try not to leave after 6:00, but I normally stay until around that time every day since we've been so busy lately." Tia answered while she was gathering her things to leave. "I'm leaving a little early today because I have an appointment for a facial."

"Oh, I'm about fifteen minutes from your office. Where is your appointment?" Sean was across town at his office but would make it to Tia in fifteen if she agreed to it.

Tia was shocked. "I'm going to this new spot Beauty Box. It's on Fifth." She wanted to see Sean but was relieved that she had a previous engagement.

"Are you serious? I know the owner of that place. How'd you hear about it?"

"It's the talk of the town right now. I hear it's really nice. I can't wait to check it out." Tia tried to keep an even tone but wondered how Sean knew the owner. Ken had met her at some NBA event and went on and on about her, a young chick from New Orleans.

"I guess I'm out of the loop. I haven't heard, but that's a good thing. Shuwan, is a good girl. She's dating my boy. In fact, he moved her here, so I'm thinking they'll get married soon. You mind if I meet you over there? I haven't seen the place since they opened, and I would love to see you." Sean was excited now. His boy, Dennis had been in the NBA for five years before he got injured. Although he was still within his contract, Dennis knew that his chances of playing again were slim and started investing in real estate. Shuwan was young, but smart and her dream of owning a day spa fell right in line with Dennis's plan for financial security. The two of them had been asking Sean to stop by ever since he missed the grand opening. He knew that Shuwan would be happy to see him.

"I don't have a problem with it. I won't be there for about thirty minutes and my appointments in forty-five, though" Tia was nervous. She had not really expected to see Sean again so soon.

"I'll see you there." Sean hung up before Tia said anything. He didn't want her to change her mind. The spa was only about 10 minutes from his office which was great because he wanted to get there before she did.

Sean walked into Beauty Box and was extremely impressed. The place looked hot; very feminine and classy. He was greeted by a nice-looking receptionist with a welcoming smile. Sean told the receptionist his name and asked if the owner was in. The receptionist asked Sean if there was anything that she could help him with, and he explained to her that he was a friend stopping by to say hello. Tasha seemed relieved that Sean wasn't there to complain and picked up the telephone. He heard her tell someone that he was here and saw a smile appear on Tasha's face before hanging up the phone.

"Shuwan would like me to show you to her office. She was happy to hear that you're here." The receptionist sounded as if she wanted an explanation for Shuwan's happiness.

"Good. Thanks." Sean followed Tasha and ignored the pry.

Shuwan stepped outside of her office to meet Sean looking as stunning as ever. She was wearing a black, wrap dress that fit her perfectly. Sean was sure that it was manufactured by some expensive designer. Her arms were outstretched, and the sleeves of the dress dangled around her wrist. "Look what the wind blew in." Shuwan said as she walked toward Sean and gave him a warm hug. "It's great to see you." She stepped back to look at him.

"The place is much nicer than you guys described it. Tight work! I really like it." Sean said flashing a smile.

"Thank you. Thank you. I'm still on a high over the whole thing. Business has been unbelievable." Shuwan grabbed Sean's hand and led him into her office. "Come in and sit down. Do you want anything? A glass of wine?"

"No, thanks." Sean said. "I'm actually meeting someone here. She should be here any minute if she's not already. I'm glad you're here. I'll come back and take you up on that glass of wine once I talk to her."

Sean looked around the office that was just as striking as the rest of the place. Her desk was a large glass sheet sitting on legs so thin that the glass looked as if it were suspended in midair. On top of the crystal clear glass sat the flat screen computer monitor, a phone and a photograph of Shuwan and Dennis looking like celebrities. There were five chairs in the room including the one behind Shuwan's desk. They were all made from a cowhide that had been dyed deep lavender. Two of the chairs were overstuffed with a small, glass table between them.

The pictures on the wall were exceptionally light, airy and tranquil. Sean saw two foot stools of the same finely dyed material and imagined his two friends having drinks and sharing dreams in the space. The place suited them. They were a great couple.

Shuwan showed her surprise at Sean's news. "Silly me" she said, "To actually think that you were coming by for a friendly visit." She was joking. "May I ask who it is?"

"A friend told me that she had an appointment here and since I wanted to stop by to see the place anyway, I thought it would be great to meet her here. She said that this is the 'talk of the town', so I'm feeling special to be in your presence." Sean laughed before he got up from his plush seat across from Shuwan. He hadn't thought about how he would present Tia to his friends. He couldn't remember ever introducing them to a female friend. Although he had them, they were never around any of his friends because they were normally related to business in some way.

"I can have Tasha send her back and you can have the office if you need privacy. There's quite a bit of traffic in the front." Shuwan got up.

"That could work because her appointment is in about fifteen minutes. I was just going to say hi to her anyway. I'll introduce the two of you. She's cool. Her name's Tia; Tia Lawson." Sean sat down and remembered how accommodating Shuwan had been since he met her. She always knew how to make people feel comfortable and was always ready to do whatever she could to help. With her, a person could not refuse, because she made it seem as if she wanted to help more than that person wanted to be helped. He was thinking about how much Dennis had changed since he met Shuwan and how much happier he seemed when he heard Shuwan's voice.

She walked into the office with Tia and said, "Surprise. I promised my friend here that I wouldn't make him miss his meeting with you, so I decided to escort you to him myself." Shuwan smiled at Tia.

Tia looked gorgeous. She was not the drop dead, model type that Shuwan was. She was only about 5' 3" while Shuwan stood about 5' 9".

Shuwan's hair was in the middle of her back and was weaved while Tia's natural hair was just past her shoulders, and she wore it back in a ponytail. Shuwan looked as if she had her own personal makeup artist and Tia's makeup was minimal. Tia wore a brown loose fitting jersey dress that was belted and pulled up to shorten the length revealing Tia's legs that looked like melted caramel. Sean smiled at the sight of the two beautiful women. He was in good company.

The puzzled look on Tia's face turned into a smile when she saw Sean. He looked handsome as ever.

Sean stood up quickly. "Hi, Tia. I guess you've met Shuwan. She's a good friend of mine; and Shuwan this is Tia."

Shuwan grabbed Tia's hand and squeezed it. "It's nice to meet you. Have a seat." She motioned to the chair next to Sean. "I'll let you two talk. Can I get you anything?"

Sean and Tia said "no" in unison.

"Okay, Tia. I'll let your technician know that you're here. If you need some extra time, it won't be a problem." Shuwan said and walked out of the office.

As soon as the door closed Tia began telling Sean how baffled she was when Shuwan asked for her. She thought that she wanted to meet her because she was a new client. She took Sean's mind away from the nervous feeling that he got when Shuwan left the room. He felt as if he were on the spot, but Tia's casual conversation relaxed him.

They made small talk for about twenty minutes before Tia said that she should go. Sean told her that he was going to stay and talk to Shuwan for a while. He hoped that she would take the bait and see him after her service, but Tia said that she needed to get home because she had to study.

Chapter Eighteen

Shuwan *was* beautiful and she seemed to be a genuinely nice person. Tia could see what Ken had been making such a fuss about. "Hi, Ms. Lawson." The receptionist said when Tia gave her name at the front desk. "The owner of the salon would like to see you; one moment."

"Hi, I'm Shuwan. Welcome to Beauty Box. I hope you enjoy the services here." Shuwan said to Tia as she walked her back to her office.

Tia felt totally relaxed during her facial. She wondered if the reason she thought it was the best facial that she ever had had anything to do with the fact that Sean was there. Her heart dropped when she walked into Shuwan's office and saw Sean sitting there looking delicious. She hoped that Shuwan's female intuition didn't pick up on what she was feeling. His skin was flawless and his smile, that smile could make a woman faint. The office was filled with the smell of his cologne when Tia walked in. The scent immediately took her back to the night before that she spent laughing and talking with Sean.

When Shuwan left the office, Tia went into a nervous chatter. She couldn't remember what she had said but hoped that she didn't sound silly. Sean's calm tone, that Tia realized was a norm for him, made Tia feel at ease. He told her more about his friend Dennis and what a fantastic couple he and Shuwan made. Sean spoke very highly of Shuwan, and Tia felt that the admiration was mutual.

Tia wanted to go talk to Sean and Shuwan after the facial, but she didn't think it was a good idea. She did want to get to know Shuwan. Sean told Tia that she had been a little nervous about the business because she didn't know many females in the area. She ended up spending major on some high-end marketing strategies that seemed to have been pretty effective.

When she was sitting talking to Sean it felt way too comfortable. She remembered leaning over to touch him a couple of times during the conversation. Whenever she did it, she would catch herself, but it was because of the level of comfort she felt with Sean. She was not up for fighting the feelings of wanting to touch him any more today.

CHAPTER NINETEEN

Ken felt much better after having lunch with Jake. He realized that it was just the shock of the news that initially had him so flustered. When he spoke with Jake, he soon came to see that the situation was not one that he could not handle. His accountant reassured him of his financial security.

On the way back to the office Ken really had time to sort his thoughts out about his predicament. He had pressed panic and hadn't really looked at the situation. It wasn't as bad as he initially thought. Something inside him told him that Lacey would be an excellent mother although he never heard her speak about having her own children. She would stop and goo goo with babies on the street. *She was so loving and attentive; yeah, she would be a great mom*, Ken thought.

He had wanted to be a dad for the longest time and had finally put it on the backburner. He decided that it would happen when the time was right. *How strange*, Ken thought. *When the time was right*. He had made the decision to stop stressing about the whole baby, family thing after he and Lacey split. He thought maybe he wasn't as ready as he thought, mentally or emotionally. He also thought that maybe

Lacey backed away because he wasn't what she expected. And now a baby.

Ken wanted to see Lacey. In fact, he couldn't wait to see Lacey and decided to go over to her place. He didn't normally go there and never unexpectedly, but this was different. Lacey didn't sound good when he spoke with her. She said that she just called because she knew that it was the right thing to do. Ken wanted to go to her immediately, but he was so caught off guard that he needed some time to get his own thoughts together. He felt better and he just wanted to comfort Lacey in any way he could.

On the drive to Lacey's, Ken looked in the backseat of his BMW and made the decision to get an SUV. He didn't want to feel cramped when he put the baby seat in the car. He kept envisioning himself with Lacey and the baby in malls, visiting relatives and going to church. He was smiling.

When Ken pulled up to Lacey's house, he got nervous again. He hoped that she wouldn't be upset about him stopping by unexpectedly. He sat in his car for a few minutes trying to think of what he would say when he saw Lacey. He said a quick prayer before getting out of his car.

Ken rang the bell and waited anxiously. When there was no answer, he rang again. "Coming." He heard someone say. It made him feel better because Lacey's voice sounded clear; much different than she sounded when he spoke with her a couple hours before.

When the door opened, Ken was surprised to see Lacey's mother. It had been a while since he had seen her, but she looked much older than he remembered. He wondered if she was sick or something. He had almost forgotten that Ms. Cooper lived there because Lacey hadn't mentioned her in such a long time. He immediately felt terrible because he hadn't even asked her how her mother was doing in the longest time.

"Hi, Ms. Cooper." Ken said. "Is Lacey here?"

She looked at Ken as if she weren't sure who he was. "Yeah. Who should I tell her wants to see her?"

"Can you tell her it's Ken? Please." He said realizing that she didn't remember him. He thought that maybe he had mistaken her for being sick. He thought that she looked as if she had been drinking way too much.

"Ken." She said and walked away leaving him standing on the front porch. He could hear her yell Lacey's name as she left. "Someone is here to see you."

After what seemed like forever, although it may have been only five minutes or so, Ken could see Lacey coming through the glass on the French doors. She was a mess. When she got to the door, she stood there with her arms clutching her waist looking at the floor for a moment. Ken thought that he saw her body shake as if she were sobbing and he thought that he would have to bust in the door. But when he touched the knob, he was relieved to find the door unlocked. He opened the door and grabbed Lacey.

Ken held Lacey in his arms and they both cried. "It's ok." He whispered in her ear. "I promise you; everything is ok."

He felt better just being there with her. The vision of her made it clear for him and Ken knew for sure that things were going to work out. He didn't know this side of Lacey. She was always independent and strong when he was around. She handled her business and never complained to him about anything. He could have been intimidated by that, but he wasn't, and he enjoyed comforting her in this moment.

The more Ken assured Lacey that he would be there no matter what and that it would be okay, the more she bawled.

Finally, he took Lacey's hand and led her into her living room to have a seat on the sleek white leather sofa. They both sat and Lacey looked up at Ken for the first time since he had been there. When their eyes met, Lacey began crying again. Ken didn't want to cry anymore, but he was taken aback by the pain he saw in Lacey's bloodshot eyes. Her eyes were swollen, and her makeup was smeared making her look as if she had two black eyes, but the pain that Ken saw hurt him to his heart.

"I'm sorry." Were the first words that Ken heard Lacey say through her tears. "I'm so sorry."

Lacey's head was in Ken's lap, and he was stroking her hair. "Sorry? There's nothing to be sorry about, Lacey. Nothing."

She laid there quietly for a while and Ken thought that she had fallen asleep. He could not understand what was happening. He hadn't given the proper consideration to Lacey's standpoint. He reacted as if he were a victim without considering the other adult's life that would also be altered. *Hell,* Ken thought, *I don't even know if Lacey wants to have the baby. 'Sorry'? Where did that come from?* he asked himself. All types of things crossed his mind while he sat there enjoying the strange closeness with Lacey. Maybe she was sorry because she called him prematurely and there were other potential fathers. *Was she sorry that she hadn't used any precautions? Neither had I,* Ken thought. Was it because she didn't plan to go through with the pregnancy? He felt a fresh tear roll down the side of Lacey's face.

He couldn't take it anymore. "Baby, please talk to me." He lifted her face so that he could see her weeping eyes.

"Please stop crying, we can get through this. You just need to relax for a while and get your thoughts together. Sometimes the shock factor is bigger than the actual issue." Ken tried to brush Lacey's hair back with his hand. The gesture was meant more to comfort her than anything else.

"Have you eaten anything?" Ken asked.

Lacey just shook her head to say, no.

"Ok. Why don't you go lie down for a while? I'm going to run out and get something to eat. You want some soup?"

"Ok." Lacey said weakly and she let Ken lead her to her bedroom.

Ken walked into Lacey's large room and stood for a moment. The room was immaculate. It was a total contrast to the present appearance of the owner. The soft smell took him back to the first time he had entered her bedroom. He remembered thinking that the room was huge for a bedroom, and he wondered where the delicate scent that filled the room was coming from. Today he still wanted to know how an aroma so light could completely fill a room so large.

He led Lacey to the side of her bed. He turned the comforter back, removed her robe, and helped her into bed before he pulled the comforter back up to cover her. Lacey was wearing a beautiful black and gray panty and bra matching ensemble that Ken had to *make* himself ignore.

He looked around to see if there was anything else that he could do to make her more comfortable. "Try to get some rest. I'll be back." He said and kissed her on her forehead.

"Use the code to get in when you come back." Lacey said softly. "It's your birthday."

CHAPTER TWENTY

Wow! Tia thought when her esthetician left the room. *That was the best facial I have ever had.* She removed the plush, lilac robe and began to redress herself. At first, she thought she may have overrated the place because of Sean and the celebrity treatment she had gotten on his behalf. But the facial had come with a mini massage *and* an eyebrow touchup. No wonder everyone was talking about Beauty Box. Shuwan had left no stone unturned. Tia's skin felt like butter, and she could not think of one thing that would have added to the experience.

After she checked herself out in the mirror, Tia walked out feeling good about herself and the spa that she knew she would be frequenting. She floated to the reception area to take care of her bill and quietly wondered what the price was for so much pampering.

Tia handed her American Express to the pretty girl who was waiting for her in the checkout area. Her nametag read Tamiki. "Did you enjoy your treatment?" She asked, accepting Tia's card. She went to the computer and typed in Tia's name.

"Did I?" Tia answered. "It was great." She flashed a genuine smile to assure her that she meant what she said.

"Would you like a drink before you leave? Coffee, tea..."

"Oh, Ms. Lawson," Tamiki said "your bill has already been taken care of." She handed the card back to a puzzled Tia.

"Really? Are you sure?" Tia asked hoping that Sean hadn't paid her bill.

"Yep. Your balance is zero." Tamiki smiled as if she herself had just made a great experience greater.

"Well, alrighty then." Tia replied trying to sound happy. She took one of the pinKenvelopes that had Anelia professionally scripted on it in purple and stuffed a twenty-dollar bill inside. She handed it to Tamiki, thanked her and walked out feeling lightheaded.

Tia hurried to her truck, pushed the button to unlock the door when she was a couple steps away and quickly got inside. She sat in the driver's seat and leaned her head back on the headrest. *Whoa!* She thought. So much had happened in such a short space of time that it was hard for her to process everything. She picked up her cell phone and dialed Zena.

Tia and Zena had been tight since forever, however Zena and Carl had become close over the years. They had a mutual love and respect for each other. Zena was a very loyal person. Although she was Tia's best friend, Tia had decided that she wouldn't tell her so much to make her uncomfortable around Carl. Now she would have to revoke that decision because she needed to hear someone else's thoughts.

She had talked to Zena about Sean, but now Tia needed Zena to *feel* her. She had to tell her everything. About how she couldn't stop thinking about Sean, and how she got butterflies whenever she heard his voice. She couldn't keep trying to do this by herself. It was becoming too much for Tia to handle, especially alone. Now with all the twists and turns that were being added Tia knew that she needed her friend.

"Hey girlie." Zena answered cheerfully.

"Hey. I hope you aren't busy because I need you."

"Perfect timing, I'm just polishing my toenails." Zena remained calm although she thought she heard panic in Tia's voice.

"Good. Don't say a word, just listen." Tia began telling her friend everything she could think of about her and Sean. She included all the fine details, down to the way the smell of Sean made her weak in the knees. She finished by telling her what had just happened at Beauty Box, and she was mentally exhausted.

"Wow!" Zena said when it was finally her turn to talk. "That shit is sexy!" She almost screamed into the telephone.

That got a smile out of Tia. "What?" She screamed back. "You fool, I called you so you could tell me to take my dumb ass home, make dinner, change my number and delete his ass from every hard drive I have."

"Oh. Was that what I was supposed to say? Ok. Do all that. But how much did that facial cost him?"

"I don't know! That's what I mean. I can't accept money or gifts from him, and I'm offended."

"Well, remember you're talking to someone who is at home alone painting her own nails."

They both laughed and, as usual, Tia felt better after talking to Zena. She still didn't have any answers, and Zena agreed that the whole ordeal was mind-blowing.

They talked while Tia drove home and both decided that Tia would have to keep Sean around long enough for Zena to meet him. She would be coming for a visit in a month and neither of them knew if they could wait that long to see each other.

Tia could not remember when she had been so happy to see Carlton and Tianna. She went home and fell into her children's world until they were both fast asleep. Then she had to find a way to deal with Carl. For the first time since she met him, Tia felt that communicating with her husband was a task. It seemed as if they were having the same conversation that they had the day before, and the month before, and the month before that. Her responses were thoughtless because she could not stop thinking about Sean.

While lying in her bed that night, Tia decided that she would take Sean out for a nice dinner to repay him for the facial and she would explain to him the boundaries that she expected for their friendship. She knew that Sean would be surprised when she invited him out for dinner, but Tia figured that would be a mature way to handle it. She would try to make it extra nice and hopefully take him somewhere he had never been.

CHAPTER TWENTY-ONE

Lacey couldn't sleep. She couldn't shed another tear. She didn't have any more tears to shed. She laid in bed and felt lifeless. The only thing that moved was her thoughts. Lacey tried to give her brain a break, but it didn't work. She was used to being in control so she couldn't stop thinking about how her situation was going to pan out.

She wished that she could take everything she owned and just move away, have her baby and live her life. However, rational thinking came, and she knew that could never work for many reasons, so she had to find a way to make things work for herself and her baby first, then for everyone else involved.

Lacey knew that Ken would not consider being absent from his child's life and that made the situation exceedingly difficult for her. She made her own decisions, and she did not want to have to consider or consult with anyone when it came to making decisions about her child.

She thought about having that conversation with Ken. She would tell him that she didn't need or expect any financial contribution from him, and she would allow him to spend a reasonable amount of time with their child, but all decisions would be left to her. She would assure him with a legally binding contract.

Her head pounded even more when the reality hit her that Ken would never go for it, and she heard him walking into her house.

The sound of someone coming into her home while she laid in bed was strange. Lacey's mom rarely left the house without Lacey unless she was on one of her binges. When she went out on a binge, Lacey would either go get her from some of the most ungodly places that one could imagine, or she would be pacing the floors waiting for her to come home. But today she was in bed, confused, and so she just lay there and waited while she heard Ken's footsteps coming closer down the long hallway to her bedroom.

When she opened her eyes, Ken was standing there, in the doorway of Lacey's bedroom, with a flower arrangement in one hand, a shopping bag from her favorite soup and salad spot in the other hand and a look of concern on his face that made Lacey melt inside. Ken smiled when he noticed that Lacey's eyes were opened.

"Hey. I got soup from the best place in town, but I didn't know what kind you like so you have a variety to choose from." Ken walked over to the dresser and sat the vase of flowers right in the center. Then he walked over to Lacey's bedside and looked inside the shopping bag. "They also have great breads, so we have that too. Would you like broccoli and cheddar, chicken and wild rice, or chicken soup for the soul?"

Lacey was weak but she found the strength to respond. "That's my favorite soup joint. All of the soup is good, but I think I better take the chicken soup for the soul and I'm hoping it's really just chicken noodle."

"Okay. Do you think your mom wants some? There's more than enough here." Ken asked sincerely.

"I don't know. She might. Can you warm the soup for me please? I like it really hot." Lacey said softly. "There are some trays in the kitchen and if you see Mom ask her if she wants any. If not don't worry about

it."

"Your wish is my command." Ken said as he turned to go to the kitchen with the bag full of soup and bread. The funny thing is that he really meant it when he said it.

There was no movement in the house and Ken wondered if Ms. Cooper was still there. He went into the kitchen and found a bowl for Lacey's soup. He put it in the microwave and remembered that he hadn't brought anything to drink. He opened Lacey's refrigerator and thought about the fact that he had never done that before. He didn't even know what types of things Lacey kept in there and was surprised to find a variety of drinks, sodas, juices, water and a couple bottles of wine.

CHAPTER TWENTY-TWO

*H*i Sean. It's Tia. Give me a call when you have time, okay? I want to ask you something.

Sean had already listened to Tia's message twice. This was the third time he replayed it. He heard something different in her voice and it made him uneasy. *Ask me something,* Sean thought as he dialed Tia's number. He didn't talk to her the day before because she hadn't answered any of his calls and he was puzzled by her message.

To, his surprise, Tia answered on the first ring.

"Hey, you", Tia said when she picked up. She had been waiting for Sean's call. "What's up?"

"You tell me. I thought you were missing in action." Sean felt his worries ease once he heard Tia's voice. He thought she sounded happy to hear from him.

"No. I was really busy yesterday, but I also wanted to give you some breathing room." Tia didn't know where the last part had come from but the fact that the two of them had talked for hours every day for the last couple of weeks did concern her.

"Breathing room? What does that mean? My breathing's fine." Sean really didn't understand what Tia meant and wanted her to explain.

Tia wanted to take the words back as soon as she heard Sean's response, but couldn't. So, she had to deal with it. "Well, it's just that we've been talking every day for the last couple of weeks and…I don't know." Tia didn't really know what to say.

"And *yes*, I am getting used to it; and I'm enjoying it. Whenever that stops, I won't be blowing up your phone like I was yesterday. Okay? You were a 'little busy'. I'll take that. If you want 'breathing room' as you call it, you'll have to say that. As for me, well let's just say, that is not what I want from you." Ken said before he thought about it. He would have never said so much if he had thought first, but he felt better after saying it.

"Uh, okay." Tia spoke slowly trying to conceal her shock from being heard in her voice. "I was really joking about the breathing room. I mean I know that we may not be able to talk every single day, so I guess I'm trying to save myself. I enjoy the conversations that we have, obviously." Tia stopped herself before she began rambling. "Which is one of the reasons why I was wondering if you have any plans for this weekend?"

"Uh, actually I don't have any plans for the weekend." Sean was caught off guard by Tia's quick flip. "Why? Did you want to make some?" He wanted her to know that he was up for whatever.

"Well, I was hoping that I could take you out to repay you for what you did the other day."

Now he was really puzzled. "What I did the other day." He repeated the words slowly trying to jog his memory. "What did I do?" He asked.

"Yeah, right Sean. You know what you did, and since we're talking about it, I can tell you that I wasn't comfortable with it." Tia thought that this may be a good time to talk about some boundaries.

"What?" Sean asked, seriously shocked.

"The facial, Sean." Tia answered flatly. She thought she heard some irritation in his voice.

"The facial?" Sean could not figure out what Tia was talking about.

"Yes, the facial. Why are you being silly?"

"I'm not being silly. I have no idea what you're talking about. Unless…" Sean thought about Shuwan. Knowing her she probably upgraded Tia's service and Tia thought that it was his doing. "What happened with your facial?"

"Are you serious?" Tia paused. "When I went to pay for my facial at Beauty Box, the receptionist told me that it had been taken care of. I assumed that you paid for it." Tia was a bit puzzled herself now.

Sean smiled at the thought of his friend. She is something else, he thought. "Shuwan must have done that. She didn't say a word to me about it either. I'll have to call her after I accept your apology." Sean smirked. *Tia had been ready to put me in my place,* he thought.

"Well, that was very nice of her." Tia said honestly and smiled about Sean's remark. "I'm definitely going to go there again. I'll have to thank her. You guys must be awfully close."

"Yeah, they're good people. Wait until you meet Dennis, he's just as cool." Ken wondered what happened to the apology and said, "Oh, does that mean that you aren't taking me out this weekend?"

"Weeeellllll?" Tia said, playfully.

"Well, guess what. I would never let you do that, so it's a good thing that it was Shuwan and not me. I got the vibe that you weren't that type so I wasn't really thinking along those lines." Sean thought that Tia seemed self-sufficient although they had never talked about their personal finances.

"What type?" Tia asked wondering what Sean meant.

"You know, the type of person that's looking for a handout." Sean thought that was a good explanation.

Okay, Tia thought, *that's not bad.* Before she got married, Tia was definitely "the type". She measured how a person felt for her by the things they gave her. Looking back, she could see that those things were small, e.g., clothes, purses and some jewelry that didn't add up to much. She wondered where her head had been.

"When I give you something, I don't think you would be able to repay me anyway." Sean laughed at his frankness. "I mean I wouldn't want you to."

"I'm glad you cleaned that up." Tia said. "I was about to be offended."

"No, I'm laughing because I know that sounded funny." He stopped laughing and said, "I don't know if I'm right or not, but you don't come off like you want things like that." He laughed again when he really thought about it. "That's why you tried to return that facial so quickly. You were like, 'negro please, I can pay for my own facial!'"

Tia laughed.

"So, I know what that means." Sean said in his normal confident voice.

"What?" Tia asked, smiling.

"You like the big stuff."

Tia felt her panties get wet. She had to stay far away from Sean.

CHAPTER TWENTY-THREE

The hot soup soothed Lacey's stomach and she began to think more clearly. She knew that she had made the right decision by calling Ken and she felt good being with him. He was being so thoughtful and comforting. Lacey thought again about how he would react when he found out that she was going to go through with the pregnancy.

"The soup is delicious. I really appreciate it. Everything." Lacey hesitated. "I didn't want to upset you today; it's just that...I didn't know who else to call." Lacey felt the tears coming.

"Baby really, you *alarmed* me. I have never heard you sound like that before. But as far as the news you gave me, it was a surprise. I had a thousand thoughts running around in my head. After the shock of it all, the very first thought that I had was of you carrying my child. I don't have a word for what I felt, but it was far from upset." Ken was being totally honest with Lacey. "I don't know if you want to talk about it right now, but why were you apologizing to me earlier?"

Lacey could not stop herself from crying while Ken talked to her. She wanted to tell Ken everything, but she knew that if she tried to talk, she would just cry more. Lacey got out from underneath the covers of her bed and walked over to where Ken sat. She sat next to him and put her head on his shoulder.

Ken embraced Lacey. He kissed the top of her head. Lacey looked up into Ken's eyes and he was helpless. He kissed Lacey so passionately that he was oblivious to everything else. He stroked her back through the thin robe until he couldn't take it anymore. He desperately pulled at the loosely tied belt until it opened, and he could get feel Lacey's smooth skin.

Lacey melted into Ken's embrace. She welcomed his tongue in her mouth when he came in to kiss her. Lacey held Ken's face so that he couldn't stop kissing her. She wanted to make love to him. When Ken untied her robe, Lacey dropped her shoulders and let it fall to the floor. She wanted to feel his hands on her body. She pushed Ken gently so he would lie back on her chaise lounge.

Ken's hands went down the small of Lacey's back and around the curve of her firm ass across the lace panties and back up again. She was on top of Ken, and he thought he would explode. Before he realized it, Ken was gripping Lacey's ass, pressing her against his body.

Lacey began to roll her body on Ken. She wanted to feel him. She began to slide her panty down. She got them across her gyrating ass and Ken slid them the rest of the way down her legs. He was fully dressed, but Lacey was burning for him, and she wanted to be naked. She began to slide her bra straps down her arms and Ken skillfully helped her with the rest. When Lacey was completely unclothed, she unbuttoned Ken's shirt and let her nipples brush through the hair on his chest. She loved the way his skin smelled. She didn't stop moving her hips. Lacey opened her legs and slid up and down Ken's leg. When she couldn't take any more of the jeans, she began to unbuckle Ken's belt. He tried to help, but she pushed his hands away. She kissed and licked Ken's body wherever her lips stopped while she glided her wet clitoris up and down Ken's thighs.

Lacey completely undressed Ken while he lay on the chaise. When her fingers finally reached Ken's erect dick, the tip was dripping precum. Lacey could not wait any longer. She sat on top of Ken and slid slowly down his penis and back up. His dick felt so good going in and out of her. Her eyes were closed, and she felt Ken sit up and wrap his arms around her like he was holding on for dear life. That movement put Ken's chiseled stomach right up against Lacey's swollen clit. She felt like every part of their bodies was working in unison. They both exploded and slept with their bodies entangled for the rest of the night.

CHAPTER TWENTY-FOUR

Tia looked around The Grill and wondered what made everyone there seem to be so happy. It was a very trendy place in the downtown area, and it was packed. Everywhere she looked people were laughing and talking. She focused on two men who sat at the bar; whatever they were talking about seemed deep. They didn't notice anything else around them as they leaned in close to each other and talked and listened, one of them talked with his hands and the other moved his face back quickly to miss the hit. She smiled to herself, lost in her surroundings. Tia liked the atmosphere and couldn't believe how comfortable she felt.

"Every time I come here; I try to figure out what it is that attracts so many people to this place." Sean said when he noticed Tia checking the place out.

"I don't know, but I've heard a lot about it. How's the food?" Tia wasn't really hungry although she hadn't eaten all day.

"It's a'ight." Sean tried to sound urban. "I don't think it's the reason that people come here, but it's not bad."

"It's in a great location and the décor is really trendy. Why do you come here?" Tia asked.

"I guess to understand what all the hype is about. You want to order some food?" They were drinking apple martinis and Sean had forgotten to ask Tia if she was hungry. "I should eat something. I haven't eaten since this morning. You got me off my square; I'm not even hungry." Sean fessed up.

Tia looked at Sean to try to see if he was joking. She was shocked because she was thinking the same thing. This man had her all discombobulated! She needed to eat because she knew that she couldn't handle drinking on an empty stomach, but she did not have an appetite. "Off *your* square? I'm out here having drinks with you on a Saturday evening, basically on lover's lane and you're off your square? I must be off my rocker." Tia smiled, but once she said it the realization came.

He had called Tia just as she was leaving the hair salon. He told her that he was thinking about going by Beauty Box to thank Shuwan. The hair salon was only about fifteen minutes away, so Tia asked if he minded if she met him there. She also wanted to thank Shuwan. Sean thought it was a great idea.

He pulled into the parking lot about two seconds after Tia. He caught her doing her last-minute mirror check. Shuwan seemed genuinely happy to see them both. When they both thanked her for the kind gesture Shuwan looked up at Sean, said "Oh please" and gently tapped him on the arm. Then she looked at Tia and said "He has come through for us so many times that I had to jump at the opportunity to return the favor. Plus, I wanted to make sure that you come back."

"I will definitely be a client, but you didn't have to do that." Tia could see why Sean liked Shuwan so much. She was really charming.

Shuwan got in between Sean and Tia. She laced her arms between both of theirs and said, "Come, you're not going to believe this."

They walked to her office with her and Shuwan flung the door open to find an extremely handsome man leaned back in her desk chair with his feet on her sleek desk and the phone in his hand. He turned and showed a look of pleasant surprise when he saw that it was Sean. "Bro, I gotta go. Sean just walked in. I'll call you tonight." Dennis said to the person on the other end of the phone.

The two of them hugged and said a couple of things that were unintelligible to Tia before Dennis said. "You gonna introduce me to your friend, Shuwan?"

"This is Tia, the one that I told you about." Shuwan answered him in a sweet voice.

Dennis, Tia and Sean looked puzzled.

"She met Sean here the other day." Shuwan reminded Dennis.

"OOOOOOH. I'm sorry. I'm Dennis. It's nice to meet you. These two have so much going on that I can hardly keep up." Dennis said as he grabbed Tia's hand and gave it a squeeze.

"It's no problem." Tia smiled. "Nice to meet you, too."

"Yeah, this is a good friend of mine. I have been telling her about you guys. So now you see the whole package." Ken said to Tia as if he wanted a response.

Shuwan brought out wine glasses, a bottle of Pinot Grigio and began to pour. They all sat and talked until the bottle was finished and Shuwan got up to get another. Sean would not let her open the second bottle and promised that we would all get together again. He talked privately with

Dennis while the two ladies continued to get to know each other.

Tia told Shuwan about how the free facial turned out. Afterwards she wondered if she had said too much. She hoped that Shuwan hadn't read anything between the lines.

Sean told them all that he and Tia had to leave because they were going to grab a bite to eat. Tia was surprised because they had not discussed doing anything, but she thought it was sexy that Sean took it upon himself to make that decision for her.

When they were outside, Tia tried to protest but Sean walked her to his car, opened the door, and said, "Get in."

Tia enjoyed being in the company of a man that knew how to take charge, but she had already been gone for quite a while and had no idea what she was going to say to Carl. She didn't like to lie and normally didn't have to because she didn't normally explain her goings and comings, but she had already been gone from her house for quite some time and she knew that she would need to address her absence. Once Tia began to throw lies out of her head because they didn't sound real, she began to get upset. Then she began to think that what she once thought was sexy in Sean was really disrespect. She was deep in thought and didn't realize where they were. She wondered how long they had been driving. She wanted her car. *How dare he decide for me without consulting me? He knows I have a family; he could have at least been considerate of my children,* Tia thought angrily as she felt the car stopping. She didn't know where those thoughts were coming from.

They stopped in front of a restaurant that sat right on the water. There was a pier next to the restaurant and Tia wondered what was on Sean's mind. "Okay, I know that you probably have to go so if you want, we can grab a bite to eat at the bar or the restaurant depending on the time that you have. If not, I've always wanted to take a walk out on that pier, or we can just leave, but it's beautiful out here around this time. I apologize for kidnapping you, I didn't want to say 'bye' to you at the salon."

Tia was relieved that Sean mentioned her situation, although she realized that he had already gotten what he wanted. She thought about the choices that Sean had laid out for her, and she would have loved any of them except the part about leaving. She had been away from home for an abnormal amount of time. She wasn't hungry, but the restaurant was beautiful. "You know what, you're right." Tia said. "I do need to get home, but I'm going to take you up on that walk because I've never really been out on a pier; not a long one like this. But I can't stay long." Tia threw that in because she knew that they could easily end up there for another couple of hours if they weren't careful.

CHAPTER TWENTY-FIVE

Carl couldn't believe that another episode of *the same Disney show* was coming on. This was Carlton and Tianna's latest favorite show and they had already watched two episodes: one of the parents taking their eight children to Disney World and another of a birthday party for the sextuplets. He wondered what could be next.

"When is Mommy coming home?" Carlton asked again.

"She should be home soon. I really thought that she would've been here already, but I'm here. What can Mommy do for you that Daddy can't do?" The children had questioned him several times about their Mommy's whereabouts.

"She's been gone a long time." Tianna added as a PSA.

Carl knew that Tia was probably out on one of her shopping sprees with her girls. She would normally come in with just one bag after an expensive day of shopping and Carl would think that she had done minimal damage. He later found out that the one bag would be stuffed with sometimes more than $1,500.00 worth of merchandise from various stores. Tia felt it was better than coming in the house with five or six bags inscribed with names that Carl equated with high prices. He would see her wearing the items later and, more often than not, he would just let it slide.

Tia seemed distracted lately. Carl didn't know what was bothering her, if anything, but shopping cured every ailment he had ever known Tia to have.

Carl enjoyed spending time at home, just lounging around, with the kids. They had played outside for a while earlier in the day. He had taken them to Steak 'n Shake for lunch; it was their favorite place to go without Mommy because she didn't like it as much as they did. Then Carl lost almost two hours playing on the X-Box with his two children. He made them his famous spaghetti and meatballs for dinner before bathing them and settling down for the evening.

Carl had dozed off on the couch and Carlton was fast asleep on his chest and Tianna was fast asleep with her head resting on Carl's stomach. He jumped when heard a noise in the bathroom. Then he heard the water turn on and he knew that it must have been Tia. *She must have been drinking and couldn't make it to the upstairs bathroom,* Carl thought as he tried to get up without disturbing the children too much.

He met Tia coming out of the bathroom and this time it was her turn to jump. "Oh, hey." Tia said nervously. "Where did you come from?"

"The kids and I must have fallen asleep on the couch." Carl confessed.

"Is everything okay?"

"Yeah; yeah, you just startled me." She tried to regain her composure.

"You startled *me.*" Carl said, a little sarcastically. "You never use this bathroom. You must have been drinking."

"Drinking? Do I smell like liquor?" Tia felt a wave of paranoia when she spoke and wondered if her eyes revealed what she felt. "I had some wine earlier; nothing heavy. Are the kids still on the couch?" She needed to change the subject.

"Yeah. You wanna help me with them? If not, I'll get them."

"No. I'll help."

They walked over to where their children slept peacefully. Tia grabbed Tianna and the little girl wrapped her arms around her mother and smiled without ever opening her eyes. Carl grabbed Carlton and they all went upstairs. They tucked their children comfortably into their beds and gave them both loving kisses before Carl said, "They must have thought you deserted them today. I don't know which one asked for you the most."

"I know. I had no idea that I would be gone all day. I guess I lost track of time." Tia grabbed her husband's hand and they walked into their bedroom.

She was tired as ever, but Tia knew she had to take a shower. She jumped in quickly while Carl was still getting undressed. She wanted to wash up at least once before she invited him in to shower with her. Every time she moved, she could smell the traces of Sean's cologne and she definitely did not want Carl to get a whiff of that.

She had a chance to wash the important parts a couple of times before Carl entered the bathroom to pee. Tia opened the rimless shower door to let him know that he was welcome.

Carl stepped inside the steaming shower and was met by his wife's sweet lips. After running his hands down her body and across her backside, he took the cloth from Tia and turned her around. Tia's body still looked sexy to Carl, and he enjoyed just watching her. He pulled her closer and began to wash her back. Carl lingered while he soaped Tia's nice round ass. He spread her legs so that he could wash the place where his face would soon be. Carl washed Tia down to her ankles then made his way back up. He stopped momentarily to taste his wife before he ran the soapy washcloth across her shoulders a couple of times and found himself extending his arms to reach for Tia's breast. They felt so smooth all lathered and warm under the water. Her nipples were erect just the way Carl liked them. He turned her back around to face him and his mouth went straight for the two raisins that stood perky as ever.

The two of them stood in the shower, and kissed, and embraced, and touched, and licked for at least ten minutes before Tia broke away. She slid her body down the length of Carl's body until her face met with his erect penis. She held it in her hands and rubbed it across her face. She ran his hardness across her cheeks, and she touched her closed eyelids with the tip of Carl's dick. When Tia engulfed Carl with her mouth, not only did he hear her moan, but Carl felt the vibration of her throat on his manhood, and he could take no more. Tia gave the best head that Carl had ever gotten, but he hated the fact that she was his wife, and he couldn't just burst in her face, so he gently reached to lift her back up into his arms. Tia came up reluctantly. When she stood, she was perfectly positioned so that Carl's dick was right between her legs, pressed against her clitoris. Carl pulled Tia closer, and she slightly pulled away again and again causing a sweet friction for them both. The head came close to Tia's wet, juicy hole and Carl tried to push it in, but Tia wouldn't let him. She got off on the whole anticipation thing. When she was ready, she let just the head slip inside her, and she would wind on it a couple times before letting it slip out and be caught by her thighs. Carl didn't know how Tia could stand it. He wanted to be inside of her.

Carl's dick was so hard that it was almost painful, and Tia's juices were flowing so much that Carl could feel more of her slippery liquid between her legs than the water coming from two shower heads. When he could take no more of Tia's teasing, Carl firmly turned Tia around so that his dick was now in position to slide up and down the crack of her ass. He pushed his penis inside of his wife so forcefully that he would have been sorry if it hadn't felt so good. They both moaned in unison and almost collapsed in the shower.

"Mommy, Daddy! Mommy, Daddy! Uncle Craig's coming!" Tianna and Carlton screamed as they burst into their parent's bedroom.

Carl and Tia were sprawled across the bed, on top of the fluffy down filled comforter in the raw. They both jumped up and grabbed the closest pillows to cover themselves and their nakedness. "Uncle Craig?" Carl asked.

"Yes. We saw him drive up." Tianna answered.

"Okay, I'm coming." Carl said through his grogginess.

"Go and tell Uncle Craig that Daddy's coming, okay?" Tia whispered to her children to get them out of the room.

"Don't open the door though." Carl said as they were leaving. Craig didn't normally come over so early. He hoped everything was alright as he stood to get some sweats.

"What's Craig want so early in the morning?" Tia didn't know if she had thought it or asked the question aloud.

"I'm not sure. I hope nothing's wrong." Carl answered her and looked at the clock. "11:30!"

Tia raised her head slightly to see if she could get a glimpse of the clock. "What? I wonder how long the kids have been up." She still didn't know if she was talking or just thinking.

"That's crazy." Carl said as he walked out of the room shaking his head.

He went downstairs and, by the looks of things, he could tell that his children had been awake for quite some time. There were two bowls on the table, one half full of milk with cereal that was so soggy that Carl could not tell what kind it was, and the other bowl was left with only a small trace of milk. The TV was blaring and there was a trail of toys starting at the bottom of the stairs.

Carl managed to get to the front door without tripping over anything. When he looked out of the glass, he did see his brother accompanied by a beautiful, light skinned honey. He stood behind the door and opened it revealing two overly excited children.

"Hi, Uncle Craig!", the two children shouted while tugging at his pant legs.

"What's up, guys?" Craig asked with a puzzled look on his face.

"I know you aren't just waking up."

"No, but Daddy is." Carlton answered.

"Come on in." Carl said to the honey still standing in the open doorway.

"I'm Carl."

"Oh yeah, this is my brother Carl. You have to excuse me for a minute. I'm trying to figure out if I need to call the Department of Children and

Families on these fools."

The woman looked confused. "I'm Jessica, a friend of Craig's." She stuck her hand out.

Carl shook her hand. "Ignore him. You *are* going to have to excuse this mess though. My wife and I had a late night and I guess my kids had an early morning."

"I think I may need to pick you guys up on Friday nights and have you spent the weekends with me because it looks like you are being neglected over here. Mommy and Daddy are over here acting like they're newlyweds or something." Carl heard Craig saying to his children.

"Newlyweds, what's that?" Tianna asked her uncle.

"Newlyweds are people who have just gotten married." Carl butted into the conversation. He didn't know exactly how much the kids had seen when they walked into the bedroom, and he didn't want Craig to add any fuel to the flame. "Uncle Craig's just joking with you guys." "Aaaah! We want to go to Uncle Craig's house." Tianna was the first to answer.

"How 'bout you guys clean up *our* house." Carl wanted to know who this Jessica was.

"Go ahead. I might even help you guys." Craig added as an incentive.

"I'm sorry, Jessica, this is my brother, Carl. I don't know what's going on but, he and his wife are normally responsible parents so we may not have to call the people on them today." Craig was kidding around, but he had expected them to be up and moving at this time of day.

"We stopped by to see if you guys wanted to hang out. We had breakfast with Mom, and she said that she was going to get you to bring the kids by to hang out with her today. We were thinking about taking the boat out since it's such a beautiful day, but you may not be able to see that with all the blinds closed."

They had made their way into the den and Carl saw Jessica looking around at the art Tia collected.

"That sounds cool. Let me check with Tia to see if she has anything planned." Carl stood to go talk to his wife. "Make yourself at home

Jessica. Craig knows how to find everything."

CHAPTER TWENTY-SIX

Lacey awoke and was still wrapped in Ken's embrace. She felt normal. She opened her eyes to make sure that she wasn't dreaming. She wasn't. She thought she should get up and shower since she couldn't seem to drag herself out of bed the day before. When Lacey tried to get up, she felt Ken tighten his grip on her body. She stayed there and enjoyed the warmth that she felt for a couple minutes before she turned to face him. Her lips were met by his.

"Good morning. How do you feel?" Ken felt good waking up with Lacey.

"I actually feel okay. I think I should take a shower and try to at least get out of this room today." Lacey didn't know what she was going to do, but she didn't want to let another day go to waste.

"Okay. Do you have something special that you want to do?" Ken asked hoping that her plans would include him.

"Yeah, I do." Lacey was thinking one thing but saying something else. "But I don't want to say another word until I put some soap and water on my body." Lacey stood up. She felt lightheaded, but she kept it moving. She had just bought herself some time to think. She had to tell Ken what was going through her mind. She was going to be up front and honest. She was going to tell him about her plan, her mother, and everything else; today. She did not want to go another step with him until he knew exactly what he was dealing with.

The warm water felt good on Lacey's skin. She just stood and let the water drench her while she pondered the situation at hand. She felt like crying all over again, but she couldn't. She knew that she had probably shed her last tear over this dilemma. *Now is the time for action,* Lacey thought, *the pity party is over.*

Lacey walked over to her bed with one towel wrapped on her head and one on her body. She kissed Ken lightly on the cheek to wake him. He had fallen back asleep, and he looked so peaceful.

He opened his eyes and looked at her with a smile. "Hey, beautiful." Ken's voice was soft.

"Hey. I need to talk to you. I hate to have to wake you, but I have to get this off my chest; now." Lacey was ready.

Ken immediately sat up. "What's wrong?" He asked the question then braced himself for the answer.

"Let me start by apologizing to you for this whole situation."

"Lacey, on the real –" Ken tried to interrupt, but Lacey wouldn't let him.

"When I'm done, you can say whatever you want to say, Baby. I have so many things going through my mind, and I don't want to leave anything out. So again, I apologize to you because I know how methodical you are, and this just came out of nowhere."

"Lacey –" He tried to interrupt again, but Lacey put her hand up signaling him to keep quiet. It made Ken sick to hear her say that.

"I didn't think that I could get pregnant which is why I have always been so evasive whenever the subject of children was mentioned. However, I was wrong for not being straightforward about that." Lacey went on to tell Ken how she would understand if he didn't want anything to do with her or her child and how she planned to take care of her child as a single parent. She thought that it was a good time to let Ken talk. But before she gave him the go ahead, she added, "Oh, and for the record I couldn't tell you when the last time was that I have slept with anyone besides you, so you are definitely the father."

"Lacey, let me start by telling you that I love you and I'm a man. I respect you for everything that you just said, but I am just as much responsible for this situation, our situation, as you are. And this will be my last time addressing this as a '*situation*' because we are blessed. No matter what road we took to get here, God has given us a gift, a blessing and we should be appreciative. You may have thought that you couldn't get pregnant, but I was pretty sure that I could. Does that mean that I owe you an apology now?" Ken asked the question but didn't wait for the answer.

"As far as me having a child and not having anything to do with it, that's a joke. No, it wasn't planned and yes, maybe I am 'methodical', but I am not shallow. I'm here. Whatever adjustments have to be made, I'll make them and that's just that." Ken pulled Lacey close to him. He felt good; like he could take on the world. Every problem that Lacey had thrown out there had been resolved in a matter of minutes.

Lacey collapsed in the comfort of Ken's arms. His words were like a soothing melody in her ears. His voice was comforting to Lacey, but she hadn't told him about her mother's addiction. Ken had an answer for everything, but Lacey knew that he wasn't ready for what she had to say.

Ken put his hand on Lacey's chin to lift her face so that he could see her eyes. "What is it?" Ken could see the worry in her face.

"It's my mother." Lacey said, making sure that a tear did not fall. She was done crying.

"Your mother?" Ken sounded relieved when he asked.

"Ken, my mother is a crackhead." Lacey spit it out. "She lies, she steals, she sucks, she fucks and does whatever else she can do to get money."

"Wait a minute, Baby. Slow down." Ken said, trying to understand what he was hearing. Ms. Cooper looked like she may have been going through some hard times, but a crackhead? Ken didn't think so.

Lacey took Ken back to the day that her and her mother had left her grandparents' house. He listened intently and Lacey could see the wheels turning in his head. When she finished talking, Ken was relaxed.

"Are you trying to run me away?" Ken asked Lacey. "Because if you are, you are going to have to come waaaaaaaay better than that." Although what he heard was surprising, it wasn't as bad as Lacey thought it was. It was a life situation and Ken was going to find a way to deal with it and to make it better.

CHAPTER TWENTY-SEVEN

"Hello." Tia answered the call quickly when she saw Zena's number. She hoped that Zena wasn't calling her to tell her she wasn't coming or anything like that. Tia could not wait for Zena to get there. In fact, lately she had been wishing that Zena would move back home. Tia knew that was selfish of her, so she never even mentioned it.

"Hey. Did I catch you at a bad time?" Zena could detect stress in her friend's voice.

"Nope. What's up?" Tia wanted to get straight to it.

"Well, I was calling to ask if you've planned anything for when I get there. I want to make sure I bring the right gear. But you sound stressed. What's up with you?" Zena knew Tia too well.

"I sound stressed?" Tia hated being so transparent. "I guess you know me too well, but I thought you were calling to tell me about some foolishness like you weren't coming or something."

"Girl, no. I'm actually getting a little excited. I haven't been home in a while so I'm looking forward to it. If my mother calls me one more time to ask about my flight, though, I'm going to lose it. She thinks that you or Rick are going to pick me up from the airport and she is not going to see me." Zena snuck the part about Rick in.

"Rick? You still talk to him?" Tia was really shocked.

"Nothing big; he was in town for a meeting last week and Mom happened to call while we were at dinner. Ever since then, she has been trying to figure out what's going on." Zena said honestly.

"Well, I don't blame her. What *is* going on? And is there any reason that you didn't mention it to me while I've been spilling my guts to you?" Tia asked.

"I was not about to mention Rick's dried up ass while you have so much juice flowing. He called a couple days before he was scheduled to be here and asked me if I would have dinner with him while he was here. Like I was going to say 'no'. Anyway, we had dinner at this swanky spot. We both drank too much, and you already know the rest." Zena was embarrassed because she had sworn to be done with him ever since he cheated on her; quite publicly while they were together.

"I can't believe that he still has power over you even though you have moved across the damn country." Tia didn't like to feel as if she was hating, but she hated the way Rick had treated her friend.

"He's been calling me nonstop since then talking the same mess about being sorry. When I told him that I would be in town, he started making plans. But I was calling to make sure that you have my flight information so that your ass will be at the airport on time." Zena gladly ended the conversation about Rick because she *was* still terribly weak for him.

"So that's why you are so eager to get here." Tia thought about what was really going on. "Of course, you wouldn't switch out since Rick is in the air. I thought he was still with that chick anyway. What is he going to do with her?" She knew that Z had detected the disgust in her tone.

"No, he said that's history, but you already know what that means. I'm not saying that I'm going to be with him, I'm just telling you what's going on. I'm free to do whatever I feel for the four days that I will be there." Zena really did sound carefree.

"Oh, because I know that you weren't going to sneak around with someone you used to live with." Tia was relieved to know that Zena wasn't *that* gone.

"Anyway, what's going on with you and Sean?"

"Same ole thing; I'm ready to drop my draws whenever I see him." Tia answered as seriously as possible but could barely finish the sentence. The two ladies cracked up with laughter.

"I hope you haven't dropped 'em." Zena managed to say through her laughter.

Silence.

"I know you didn't!!!!"

"No, but it is crazy for me right now. Because Sean, just wait until you meet him, he is the man that every woman in the room wants. And I am not saying that he is drop dead gorgeous, or tall, dark and handsome. He just has that damn swagger!" Tia screamed the last words into her cell phone. "It's crazy, but anyway, I come home all juiced from being with him, and having to use every ounce of willpower that I can find...to Carl. I come home to Carl's sit at home, unexcitable, never gonna step outside the box ass." Tia didn't even know where that description had come from.

Zena was shocked. She had just come to grips with the fact that Tia met someone and was dating (no matter what Tia called it, it was dating) someone other than Carl, but she didn't want any negative thoughts about Carl. Zena thought it was strange because Tia had never complained before, but suddenly Carl seemed to be a problem. She made a mental note to mention the sudden change to Tia if she picked up on it again.

"When I make love to him, it's not the same anymore Z. I don't know what happened, and before you even say it, it can't be Sean. He is the one that has me freaking the shit out of Carl, or at least trying to, because he will not budge. I stopped the TV on a porno the other night cause I was flipping through the channels, and it looked sexy. Do you know that when he noticed what it was, he picked up the remote, changed the channel, and never even said a word; as if I wasn't watching it." Tia was frustrated.

"Poor Carl, he doesn't know that a freak has been unleashed. Give the man a break girl." That was all Zena could say.

"We went out with Craig and this new chick the other day. Jessica, she seems okay, but *ve-ry* high maintenance. And Craig is picking up the tab for the maintenance right now. His nose is wide open; talking to Carl about the Louis luggage he just bought her. You know he was talking to the wrong one." This was news because Craig had always been playa playa.

"So, he's big-shotting," Tia continued, "we take the boat out, dock at BoatHouse, we eat and drink there and we had a really good time, but Craig and Jessica were all over each other and Carl and I barely touched each other the whole day besides holding hands every now and then. I don't know if that is normal for us, but I have never noticed it before. Maybe, it's me. It could be me. Anyway, let me go I'm depressing myself. I'll be at the airport. Love ya." Tia didn't give Zena a chance to respond because she knew that Zena wanted to stay as neutral as possible. She really did love her friend and she couldn't wait to see her.

Zena hung up the phone and thought about her conversation with Tia. She hoped this Sean was all Tia made him out to be. She knew that nothing good could come from the friendship no matter how nice he was. Carl *was* a rule follower, and Zena had always viewed that as one of his good attributes. She remembered a time when Tia had thought so too. She wished that she could say the same for Rick. He had taken a chance by cheating on Zena that didn't pay off for him. Zena wasn't sure if she would be able to forgive him, but she was considering giving it a chance. He left her for some model chick and then put it on blast, taking her around mutual friends as soon as he moved out of their condo they shared. Zena remembered the pain and embarrassment she felt when she and her friends were placed in such an uncomfortable situation. But Zena stood tall and endured with grace. The godfather job offer that Zena got, relocating her to the other side of the US, was right on time, but she got the victory when America's Next Top Model left Rick for some ball player that she met at an event that Rick had taken her to. Now she's all on TV sitting next to the player's wives and smiling at the camera. Prior to that, the relationship had been great. Rick said that he now realizes that it was a stupid mistake and that he never had feelings for the woman. He said it was all superficial and Zena almost believed him because she *was* a knock-out; Zena thought it would have been difficult for any man to resist her. The question was if Rick would do the same thing if the opportunity presented itself again.

Zena missed her mother also. She missed the comfortable surroundings of being in her mother's home although she could only stand to be there for short amounts of time. She always stayed at Tia's when she visited. Her mother's house didn't have the modern amenities that Zena had grown accustomed to, but it was home. For the first time in a long time, Zena was anxious to get home. She got up and went to her closet again to make sure that she had set aside everything that she needed for her trip.

CHAPTER TWENTY-EIGHT

"Hey, hey, anybody home?" Craig called out as he walked through his mother's house. He wondered where his mother had run off to. She didn't mention anything to him when he spoke to her earlier. Craig was hungry and was all revved up for some of his mother's good cooking.

After checking every room in the house, Craig surmised that he was in the house alone. He went into the den and turned the TV on. He thought about calling Carl to find out if he knew anything about where their mother was, but he knew that Carl was on his way over. Their mother was always home in the evenings, especially when she knew her boys would be there. Craig tried not to dwell on it, because Jessica kept telling him that he worries too much. *She's right*, Craig thought.

He couldn't believe that he had fallen for Jessica the way that he did. He actually considered spending the rest of his life with her. He was cautious for all the obvious reasons. Jessica was a spender, though. Craig had spent more money in the last five months than he did for the whole year last year. That worried him. Although Jessica made her own money, Craig suspected that she spent more of the money of the guys she has dated than her own. He had already spent his share, and Craig thought that may have been part of the reason for him suddenly thinking about long term commitments.

Jessica owned an employment agency. It was small but seemed to be lucrative. However, everything that Jessica possessed was expensive, from the office that she rented to her condo. He really didn't know how she could afford it all. Craig's cell phone rang and snatched him away from his thoughts.

"Hello."

"Yo, Mom is in the hospital. I'm on my way there now, so meet me over there." Carl tried to sound calm, but he was scared. He had never known his mom to be sick.

"What? What happened?" Craig immediately jumped up and grabbed his keys.

"I'm not sure, but she drove herself there without calling either one of us and that is a problem. Some nurse called me because she is being admitted. Apparently, Mom had my name down ICE, but there was only so much she could tell me over the phone. I don't even know if Mom knew that she called me." Carl had so many things going through his mind that he wasn't even sure that he answered his brother's question.

Craig was already in his car and driving. "Which one, where am I going?" He hoped he didn't have to turn around.

"St. Mary's. I'll see you there." Carl needed to call Tia to let her know what was going on.

Craig ended the call and thought about the conversation that he had with his mother that morning. She sounded fine, but Craig wondered if she was feeling sick then and hiding it. She had never been sick or anything, but Craig often worried about her living alone at her age. They had discussed a senior assisted living community, but their mother was totally against it.

Craig and Carl arrived at the same time. "You must have been driving like a bat out of hell." Craig said when his brother caught up to him walking into the hospital.

"You know it. I'm just hoping that it's nothing too serious. Did she mention anything to you?" Carl had been thinking about it all the way there. His mother hadn't given him any indication that something was wrong with her.

They walked up to the information desk and found out that their mother had already been moved into a room. They hurried up to room 404B.

When they got up to the room the nurse was there with their mother telling her where she was going to put her purse.

"There they are." Their mother said as soon as she laid eyes on her two children. "Can you give me my things back now, so I can leave? I didn't come here for this." She sounded upset.

"Hold up, Mom. What's going on?" Craig's question was meant for anyone who had an answer.

"They think something is wrong with me because I was tired. I came here on my way to the grocery store, I just wanted to rest for a minute. They wouldn't let me leave. Wanna run a cockamamie test." She sat up in the hospital bed and looked around for her things.

Carl went and put an arm around his mother's shoulders. "Give us a minute, Mom. We just want to find out exactly what happened before we take you home."

The nurse walked outside the room with Craig.

"Didn't I just tell you what happened? I'm tired of repeating myself. I am ready to get out of here before that doctor comes back. It was his idea to start running all these tests in the first place. They just want something to bill my insurance for because there ain't a thing wrong with me."

Carl wanted Craig to hurry up and tell him what was going on. He had a feeling that his mother was about to get belligerent. She only used the word "ain't" when she was ready to fight. "I'm sure the doctor felt that there was some justification for the tests, Mom. Was your blood pressure high when you came in?" He was treading lightly because he didn't want to set her off.

"Carl Lawson, get up, go out there and find out where the hell Craig went so I can go and get my groceries!" Althea spat the words out. Her voice got higher and louder with each word, and she was screaming by the end of the sentence.

Carl was startled by the sound of his mother's voice. He had never seen her this way before. He was relieved to have permission to leave the room, but he was worried about what was going on. He walked out into the hallway and saw Craig speaking to the doctor and the nurse that had just left the room. Carl rushed over to see what he could find out. "What's going on?" He said, more to his brother than the doctor.

"This is my brother Carl. And this is Dr. McKenzie." Craig rushed through the introduction. "He said that Mom is showing early signs of Alzheimer's."

"Of course, we aren't sure." The doctor interrupted. "But her behavior here is symptomatic of the early onset of Alzheimer's. Your brother says that she lives alone, which means that you really don't know if she has been showing any other symptoms. We've run some preliminary tests, but I think it would be a good idea for her to stay here for the night. That way we can keep an eye on her. She will probably be released tomorrow, but even so, she shouldn't stay alone until all the results come in. You may want to go in and do what you can to comfort her. She wasn't happy when we decided to admit her." He reached out and touched Craig on his shoulder before he turned to leave.

"Her behavior? What exactly happened, doctor? I know you're busy, but you're right, we didn't have a clue. So, I'm still kinda puzzled here." Carl refused to let him just walk away without telling him what he wanted to know.

"No, she was just excitable, and I wouldn't think that she was normally that way. I hope I didn't alarm you because I don't want you to worry right now. Let's just see how the rest of the evening goes and wait for the test results to come in. Ok?" Dr. McKenzie was known for his patience. "She needs to get some rest."

"Ok. Thank you." Carl wanted to talk to his brother, but when he turned to Craig, he saw a face filled with worry. Carl went and put his arm around Craig's shoulder and gave it a squeeze. "It's probably best that she stays here so we can make some arrangements."

Craig and Carl went back into the room where his mother and the nurse were. The nurse had gone back into the room when Carl came out to speak with the doctor. "You should get some rest." The nurse spoke calmly to their mother. "Oh, I think these two gentlemen are here to see you." She excused herself from the room.

"I'm sorry. I don't know what happened to me. I was fine when I left home, but I just got so tired, and I thought this was the best place for me to come. I was right up the street." She looked embarrassed. "I could have made it home. You didn't have to come here."

"Mom don't even say that. You know that neither one of us mind. We just want to make sure that you're okay."

Craig's tone was serious. "Let me help you with your things." Carl said to his mother.

"I have everything. I'm ready."

"Mom, the doctor thinks that you should stay here for the night for observation." Craig spoke cautiously. "We think it's best too."

"No, I really am fine." Althea could not believe they wanted her to *stay* in the hospital.

"Mom, you know that we wouldn't even consider you staying here if it weren't in your best interest. You need to rest and we, me, Craig and

Dr. McKenzie, need to know that you are okay before you go home."

"Here are some things that you may need." The nurse came in with a package.

Althea took the package without saying a word.

The nurse looked at the two handsome brothers, then back at their mother and she turned to walk out of the room. She knew that it would be difficult for them to leave her there alone.

"Excuse me." Craig said. "I didn't get your name."

"Sharon."

"Sharon, I'm Craig. This is my brother, Carl. I don't think we told you any of that before, but anyway, we really appreciate your help."

"Yeah. Thanks a lot." Carl added.

"It's no problem. That's what we do here." Sharon continued out of the room. She returned shortly with a pitcher of ice water and a few disposable cups. "Here you go, Mrs. Lawson. I'm going to be at the nurse's station. If you need me use this." Sharon lifted the call light that was attached to the bed rail. "I'll be your nurse for the night." Althea didn't say a word, she just sat there, on the side of the bed. "She seems nice." Carl said to Craig when she was gone.

"Yeah, but I'll just stay here. I think she'll feel better and so will I."

"You will do no such thing. I will stay here if you insist, but neither one of you will sit here in this hospital as if *you* are babysitting *me*." When Althea spoke, she sounded like the mother that they both knew and loved.

"Mom, no one is trying to babysit you. We are concerned and we want to do whatever we can to make this better for you. If you aren't comfortable with one of us staying here then fine, but we need you to rest tonight."

The two of them stayed and talked with their mother until she seemed tired. They both knew that they wouldn't get much rest that night, but Carl had to get home to Tia and the kids. Craig decided to stay at his mother's place because it was closer to the hospital.

They stopped to let Sharon know that they were leaving, and she tried to reassure them that their mother would be fine there overnight. Craig made sure that she had his cell phone number handy and told her to call him if anything happened.

"Don't worry." Sharon said again.

"She has never done anything like that before." Craig seemed to be searching his memory.

"You can't be sure that something hasn't happened that you don't know about. Your mother seems to be very self-reliant."

"Yeah, you're right. She probably would want to try to keep that to herself and hide it as long as she could. I sure hope not."

"I don't think so." Is what Carl said.

"Anyway, here's a business card; you can give me a call." Sharon handed him her card and hoped that he didn't take it the wrong way. She was honestly extending herself to Craig, and his family, purely because of her work and her compassion for older people transitioning in life.

"You do private duty?" Craig looked up from the card.

"Oh, yes. I work here, per diem, for extra money." She smiled at Craig.

"I'm sorry. I appreciate your help." Craig held the card up. "Have a good night."

"Okay." Sharon answered and turned to walk away.

Craig began to walk to catch up to Carl who had walked ahead and was speaking on his cell phone when he turned to say thanks again to Sharon.

Before he could say a word, Sharon turned and said, "We'll take good care of her.", with a reassuring smile.

CHAPTER TWENTY-NINE

K en got out of the elevator and looked forward to seeing Tia. She had called him a couple of times over the past week to inquire about his absence, but he needed her to be his sounding board once again. His life had changed drastically since the day that Lacey had given him the news. He hadn't had a chance to speak to anyone, not even his brother Charles, about what was going on and he knew he would feel some relief just from sharing his story.

Ken walked into Tia's office to find her looking like she was working diligently. Boney James was coming through the speakers on her computer, her fingers were moving quickly over her keyboard, and as soon as Ken stepped inside, the phone on Tia's desk began to ring. When she turned to answer the phone, she noticed that Ken was standing there. "Tia Lawson", she answered the call and quickly threw her finger in the air signaling Ken not to go anywhere. "Z, I'm going to have to call you back." She hung up the phone, got up from where she sat in front of the computer and walked over to close her office door.

She leaned her back against the closed door, folded her arms and said, "What is going on with you?"

Ken couldn't help but smile although, for some reason, he felt like he wanted to cry. "Man, I don't even know where to begin, T." Ken ran both his hands over the stubble on his chin and cheeks. "Lacey's pregnant."

Tia straightened her stance but was unsure about how to react. She recalled the night that the two of them were in Christopher's and they both acted as if they had moved on, so what exactly was, Ken saying? Tia thought she saw some signs of joy in his eyes, but she was still somewhat confused. "And?" Tia tried to sound quizzical.

"And I'm the father; we're having a baby."

"What?" Tia was so shocked on so many levels that she didn't know what to say. She walked over to a chair and took a seat.

Ken noticed the look of uncertainty on Tia's face, and it was like a slap in the face to him. He knew that he could count on Tia for a reality check. "I know it's a lot to swallow so suddenly, but that's what I've been dealing with. That's what's up with me right now." Ken thought about how he sounded as he spoke to Tia.

"Just wait; slow down." Tia sat quietly for a moment before she spoke again. "I thought that was done between you and Lacey." She was trying to put things together in her mind.

"I know. It was. It's a crazy situation, but it's all good. I'm actually excited now that I've gotten over the initial shock." Ken wanted Tia's approval. He knew that she would have his back, but he wanted her to be just as happy as he was. "I already know what's going through your head, T. Trust me I see it, but it's deep. You know what," Ken realized that they were going to need some time. "What are you doing later?"

"I'm not doing anything special. I'll probably go by my mother-in-law's house to see if they need me."

"Why, is something wrong?" Ken was concerned. He liked Mrs. Lawson.

"She was admitted to the hospital for observation, and she can't be left alone for a while, so we've been improvising. Between Carl and Craig, they have it under control, but I like to stay close by just in case."

"Wow. I've only been out of the loop for a couple days." Ken was stunned by Tia's news. He was off dealing with his own issues and hadn't even thought about the things that other people were dealing with.

"Try a week and things have been crazy." Tia said.

"I was going to say that we could go out for a drink after work, but I guess not, huh? I hope everything's okay with Mrs. Lawson."

"Yeah, we should know something soon."

"I don't know, we may have to shut the office down or something, because we definitely need to talk. You know I don't make major life decisions without consulting you." Ken was speaking from his heart and being truthful.

"Definitely, because you have blown my mind. I have so many questions that I don't know where to begin. Anyway, I guess I should say 'congratulations.'" Tia stood up and kissed Ken on the cheek.

"You'll make a great father."

"Thanks, T. You're the only other person that I've talked to about it. I don't even know if Lacey has told her mother."

"How is she?" Tia asked.

"We need to talk, man. That is a forty-five-minute story by itself. But she's okay. I have to go give her a call. Today is the first time that I've left her for any amount of time since I found out. Let me know if we can set something up for later."

"I will." Tia said while walking back behind her desk to sit at her computer. Once Ken was out, Tia let out a sigh. "Whew", she said out loud. No wonder he needed some time off; that was a lot to chew at one time. She sat and thought about everything that Ken had just told her and the skeptic in her thought about the last time that she saw Lacey. She bumped into her at the Galleria and Lacey was with a handsome older man. Tia hadn't thought anything about it before; she must've blown it off as being business related or something like that. She didn't even mention it to Ken before, but Tia just wasn't sure about this sudden baby-daddy thing. "Tia Lawson", she answered her ringing phone.

"Hey babe, what's up?" It was Carl.

"Oh, hi. Ken came in this morning and he..." Tia decided that she wasn't ready to share the story with Carl. "Uh, he was shocked to hear about your mom. Of course, he said to call if we need him for anything." She was thankful for the quick recover.

"Yeah, I was calling to let you know that I'm going to pick the kids up from school and go over Mom's for a while. She made me promise to bring them over today."

"She asked me about that, but I'm not sure that she's up for it. I was going to take them over there this weekend." Tia knew that her children were a handful.

"Well, I promised her, so I'll see how it goes. Mom actually seems to be back to normal, but the doctor did emphasize the fact that she needs rest." Carl had to at least let his mom see her grandchildren. "Craig will be there anyway, so there won't be a problem. We'll just hang out for a while."

"Alright, call me once you get them."

"Alright, Baby, I will. I love you."

"I love you, too." Tia felt weird when she said that. She placed the phone back in the cradle and got up to let Ken know that they had a date after work.

Tia got to the door of Ken's office and saw the back of Ken's high back, leather office chair. She figured that he was on a call, so she knocked softly on the frame of the door. Normally, she would have just walked in, but given the circumstances she didn't want to walk in on anything private.

When he swiveled around in the chair, Tia was surprised to see that he wasn't on the phone. He was taking in the lovely view that his office offered. "Hey." Ken said happily. "Come in. Why are you knocking?" He hoped nothing was wrong.

"I thought you were on the phone."

"Okaaaaay?" Ken felt like he was missing something.

"I didn't want to just walk in." Tia knew what he meant, but for some reason she felt awkward. There had never been a real first lady in Ken's life, so she didn't know how it was going to play out. He had always been accessible to her whenever for whatever. She couldn't remember ever feeling like an outsider with him or as if she were intruding; before now.

"What? What is up with you? Where's all this, uh, etiquette coming from?"

"I don't know. I haven't had a chance to absorb the fact that you're going to be a dad, so I think I'm just shocked. This one came out of left field." Tia needed to get all the facts straight before she could really react to the situation. She wanted to know why Ken was seeming to be so naïve. She hadn't seen him like this before; he was normally looking for the bullshit when it wasn't even there. "I came to tell you that I don't have to go to Carl's mom's tonight. So, I get a chance to hear all the details from the past week. We should go to Prime; we haven't been over there in the longest time."

"Great. I just told Charles about the pregnancy, and he actually sounded happy for me. I expected him to give me a hard time about it." That's what Ken had been thinking about when Tia walked in. He was wondering why his big brother didn't give him his usual skepticism. He did make a couple jokes about Ken taking so long to prove that his gun was loaded, but he congratulated Ken and sent his best to Lacey.

"He probably thought you were shooting blanks." Tia smiled at her own honesty and at the fact that Ken was still Ken; still looking for the bullshit and it wasn't even there.

Ken laughed but wondered if Tia and Charles had been talking. "Let's try to get out of here by 5:00. I have a stack of things to do, but I'll shut it down around 4:30."

"It's a date." Tia turned to leave.

"That dress is bangin'. It looks like you already had a date." Ken was only joking, but Tia did look sexy.

When they got to Prime, it was like old times. They bumped into one of Ken's old flames, Nikki, who thought she still may have a chance. She had one drink with them before she noticed that Ken wasn't giving her the feedback that she wanted. Tia and Ken talked for a couple hours and ended up ordering some appetizers. After Ken told Tia the whole story, everything that Lacey had told him, Tia was happy for the two of them. She was ready to take her position as God mother.

Ken kept hinting about something being different with Tia. She reminded him that she had changed her hair. Ken knew that but said it was more than the way she looked, even though he thought that she was dressing differently too. After she had Tianna and Carlton, Tia started dressing more conservatively. Now, Ken was starting to see the flare come back. Tia admitted to her friend that she was paying more attention to herself lately. She told him that she had more time now that the kids were not as dependent on her anymore, and that she wanted to make sure that she didn't lose herself.

"I ain't buyin' that." Ken told her. "I've been a little distracted, but give me a minute, and I'll figure it out." In the back of Ken's mind, he was thinking that he saw the signs of another man and he hoped it wasn't his brother. He was still puzzled by Charles' reaction to his news and the fact that he seemed unusually cheery. He knew Tia better than that. He was concerned because he knew his brother too and he had seen him pull off the impossible.

Tia giggled. She wondered if Carl had noticed as much, but she doubted it. "Whatever, Ken."

"Don't whatever me. You know that you can't keep anything from me." Ken flashed that big brother smile at Tia.

She knew that he was right. "Let's bask in your happiness for a little while before we get into my stuff." She didn't want Ken to try to find out anything on his own. She would let him know what was going on in her life, in due time. "And stop looking at me like that. You're embarrassing me."

"I knew it, man. You can't fool yo boy."

CHAPTER THIRTY

Tia decided to go by her mother in-law's house because it was still pretty early. It wasn't even eight o'clock, so she figured that Carl and Craig would still be over there with the kids. She was feeling good after listening to Ken's news. Tia got a call from Zena to "remind" her to pick her up from the airport. Zena could not have been coming at a better time. With everything that was happening, Tia felt like she was losing it. She hadn't given the situation with Althea the attention that it deserved, and she knew that it was going to impact her life in some way. Sean was taking up so much mind space that she couldn't think straight. She needed Z and her quick wit to help her regain some control in her life. She didn't have to be reminded that tomorrow was the day, she could hardly wait.

Tia turned on Althea's block and saw a strange vehicle in the driveway. Maybe it's one of Althea's friends, Tia thought. As she pulled up, Tia realized that the car belonged to a couple of "The Nerds", and she immediately felt stress. The last thing that she wanted was to be interrogated by Janice or Dominique, but she took a deep breath and got out of the car.

Craig opened the door and gave Tia a hug. "What's up, Sis?" He checked her out. "Nice dress."

"Thanks, Craig, how's everything?" Tia asked while walking inside to the back of the house. What was it about this dress? She knew it was nice when she bought it, but it turned out to be a real eye catcher. It was a wrap dress and Tia always felt good when she wore a wrap. She would keep this on reserve for when she needed to look hot, fast.

"Your people back there." Craig had a boyish smile on his face. He knew how Tia felt about Carl's friends.

"Yeah, I almost did a U when I realized who it was." She shot back at her brother-in-law.

"Well, it's about time." Tia heard as she hit the room where everyone sat.

"I'm fine. How are you?" Tia said to Janice quickly. She shot a quick look at Carl who was giving her the eye that said, "Please don't go off." "What's up Dominique?" Tia didn't see Althea and knew that she was in the back with Carlton and Tianna. "Hi, baby." Tia walked to Carl and kissed him on the cheek. "I hope the kids aren't driving your mom crazy." That was her excuse to get the hell out of there.

"Mommy, Mommy." Tia's two children ran into her arms.

"I didn't know that you were coming over here." Tianna said matterof-factly.

"I'm sorry I didn't tell you, Sweetie." Tia walked over to the side of the bed and gave her mother-in-law a hug and a kiss. "How are you?" Tia asked Althea. "I hope they didn't tire you out."

"Tire me out? Chile, please. Since when have my two grandbabies tired me out? I keep telling you, don't let them doctors fool you. I AM FINE. Na, where you coming from *Miss Thing*? Looking all sexy."

Tia sat beside Althea on the side of the bed. She felt uncomfortable standing where Althea could look at her straight on. Miss Thing? Sexy? Tia had never heard her use those words before.

"Who is *Miss Thing*, Mommy?" Tianna was not going to let it slide.

"Oh, Grandma's just joking, Baby." Tia answered.

"But where've you been. Carl said that you were working late. You still working over there with your friend?" Althea could smell the alcohol on Tia's breath.

"Yes, I'm still with Ken. I can't imagine working anywhere else. I think if I leave there, I'll be a stay-at-home mom." Tia didn't know where the line of fire was coming from, but she knew that she picked the wrong night to visit with the in-laws. "Let's get your things together, guys." She got up and gathered her two children. Again, they were her scapegoat to get the hell out of there.

"You don't look like no stay-at-home mom to me." Althea decided to say what she thought.

"Well, I don't think I'll ever look like that, but I came back here to see if you need me to do anything for you while I'm here." Tia wanted to defuse the tension. "If you need me to pick something up for you, I can bring it by tomorrow?"

"Tia, Carl and Craig have been here all day, everything that I needed done, they already did."

"Well okay, guys, give your grandmother a kiss." The two kids ran and smothered their grandmother with kisses. "I love you." She brushed Althea's cheek with a kiss.

"Why is Grandma mad at you?" Tianna asked when they left the room.

"I don't think she's mad. She's not herself right now." Tia whispered the half lie in her daughter's ear.

Tia walked back into the room where her husband sat with Craig and his friends. "We're going to go home so I can get them ready for bed." Tia said softly.

"They have gotten so big, Tia. They're adorable." Janice stood up to hug the kids.

"Thanks." Tia noticed that Janice had gained weight. "Is that a bulge?"

Janice's face lit up. "That's why we stopped by. Well, we called, and Carl told us about his mom, so we wanted to come and see her. We also want you guys to be the Godparents."

The words hung in the air.

Chapter Thirty-One

Zena sat on the plane with a Bailey's on the rocks and thought about the many plans that she had. She didn't know how she would do so many things in such a short period of time. Her mother wanted to cook a dinner for the family while she was there, so Zena would get to see everyone, at one time, all in one spot. She needed some one-on-one time with Tia which she would probably get as soon as she got off the plane, but Zena knew that Tia wanted her to meet Sean sometime during her stay. She wanted to at least take Tianna and Carlton to see a movie or something, but she didn't think it would happen this time. Rick had been calling like crazy. *And so on, and so on,* Zena thought.

She was startled when she felt the wheels of the plane touch down. Zena couldn't believe she had practically slept through the entire flight. She grabbed her bag and pulled out her Listerine spray. After she freshened her breath, Zena put some lip gloss on her lips and fluffed her hair. When the bell rang, she stood up quickly to move out.

When Zena walked into the airport, she immediately looked for a restroom. If she knew her girl, she knew that Tia was probably *on her way,* but not outside waiting. Her eyes met with a tall, dark skinned brother. Zena thought she was going to faint. It was Rick.

"Hey." Rick walked over and took her in his arms. "I couldn't wait to see you." He said in Zena's ear.

"I don't believe you." She pulled away. Zena was not mentally prepared to see Rick, and he was looking good.

"I really could not wait to see you, Z. I miss you; I miss what we had." He was serious. "I messed up, but I can promise you that it will never happen again."

Zena felt tears well up in her eyes. "Rick, I can't even do this right now." "Yeah, let's get your bags." Rick took her arm.

"I don't believe this, Rick. You can't just do this. I mean, I hear you. I heard you over the phone, but I can't tell you anything different than what I told you before I got here." She wanted to be firm. "Anyway, you know that Tia is going to be outside to pick me up."

"I already know. That's why I had to be one step ahead of her." Rick smiled at this small accomplishment. "I wanted to see you, to let you know that I meant everything that I've told you, and I hope you can fit me into your schedule somewhere while you're here."

Zena was shocked; she actually felt something when Rick said that. The whole no pressure thing worked for her right now. They talked until her bag came around. Rick grabbed the bag that Zena pointed to and the two of them walked outside. To Zena's surprise, Tia was outside.

"Oh, hell no! What is this?" Tia yelled out of her window when she saw Zena and Rick.

Zena rushed over to Tia who was getting out of her car. The two of them hugged like they hadn't seen each other in years. "I swear I didn't know he was coming here." Zena whispered to Tia in their embrace.

"Hey, Tia, what's up?" Rick walked over to the two women. "I just came to say 'hi' to my girl before you got to her. I know you are her first priority. I'm just trying to get in *somewhere*."

"Hm." Is the only sound Tia made when she glared at Rick.

"Oh, man, Tia, don't start trippin. I'm trying to be real with your girl." Rick was begging Tia with his eyes. He knew if she were against him, he would be fighting a losing battle.

"Whatever, Rick. If you came all the way to this airport, parked your car and stood at that arrival gate just to glimpse Z for five minutes, that's on you, but she is getting in my car in about 30 seconds and we're out. You can be real a little later." Tia gave him brownie points for the airport thing. The only time that Tia went into an airport is when she was about to board a plane.

Zena walked closer to Rick and said, "I'll give you a call later, okay?"

"Alright, go do your thing. I'm gonna be waiting for your call." He gave her a kiss on her cheek.

"It was very nice of you to come and meet me."

"I told you I couldn't wait." Rick was holding both of Zena's hands and looking her in her eyes.

"Call me."

"I will."

"Alright, T. Nice seeing you." Rick started walking to where his car was parked.

Zena got in the car and the two of them tried to hug over the middle console. They were both happy to see each other. "Girl, can you believe his ass." Zena squealed when both doors were securely shut, and she knew that there was no chance of Rick hearing her. "Does he really think that he can put his little Mack game down for a couple days and get back in like that?"

"If he saw that look in your eyes, he probably thinks so."

They both laughed.

"You make me sick." Zena joked.

"Rick should be the one making you sick. I'm just telling you the truth. You already know you can't fake it with me, Z."

The two of them hung out like old times, laughing and talking. They stopped to get their eyebrows threaded at Zena's favorite spot. Tia hadn't gotten hers done in weeks because she knew that Zena was going to want to go there. Then, Sean called and asked if they wanted to meet him for a drink so that he could meet this friend that he has heard so much about.

Tia couldn't wait.

CHAPTER THIRTY-TWO

Although Althea thought that she was doing well at hiding her illness, Craig and Carl had picked up on things that they had never noticed before. They had been spending much more time at their mother's house, so they had more opportunities to see how well she was able to, or actually wasn't able to, care for herself. Althea was more forgetful than either of her sons had ever noticed. She had misplaced her keys a couple of weeks ago and called Carl over to bring his spare. When he got there, Carl found her keys in the refrigerator next to the milk. Another time Craig found Althea in bed, fully clothed down to her shoes. When he woke her, she said she was waiting for some friend that Craig had never heard of to pick her up. She said she had just dozed off. He didn't believe she had been waiting for anyone. He had never known his mother to get picked up by anyone. She took herself wherever she wanted to go.

Carl walked into his mother's house wondering what surprises were awaiting him. The first thing he noticed was the smell of something sweet baking in the oven. His mood changed immediately, and he suddenly felt relaxed.

"Craig?" Althea called from somewhere in the back of the house.

"Nope, one better." Carl walked into the kitchen. There was a pot of corn chowder on the stove. He opened the oven to see that his mother was baking one of his favorite desserts, peach cobbler. His mother was the only person that he had ever known to make it exactly the way that he liked it; not too much filling, not to sweet and the crust that was baked to perfection. Carl couldn't remember the last time he had his mother's peach cobbler. He closed the oven and turned to go and give his mother a hug.

Althea was on her way into the kitchen. "I had a feeling you would be over here today. Where are my babies?"

"They stayed with Craig last night. I thought they would be over here by now." Carl hugged his mother. She looked great. He hadn't seen her look like that in a while. "Wow. You look good, Mom."

"You say that like it's a surprise."

Carl chuckled at his mother's quick response. "I guess you caught me off guard. You got the kitchen bangin' so I didn't expect you to have time to get yourself all spiffy too. What's up with all the cooking?"

"I knew you and the kids would be here and I have a friend that's stopping by, so I wanted to have a little something. You know once I get started, it's hard to stop. I'm going to make a salad and fry some chicken. How did Craig end up with the kids?"

"I'm not even sure. He promised them that they could stay over, but I didn't take him seriously. I think he may be trying to impress Jessica." Carl replied still shocked by his mom. She seemed to be back to normal and it was strange. "Who's coming by?"

"You don't know this gentleman. He's a member of the Sr.'s ministry at church. He heard about my cooking and, of course, he wants to try it. I finally decided to let him come over. You know my heart goes out to anyone that doesn't get a good, home-cooked meal every now and again."

Now Carl was really surprised. He couldn't remember the last time his mother had a male visitor, but he was sure it was a family member. He decided not to make too much of it, and just see how it played out. He heard someone coming through the door and knew it had to be Craig and the kids.

Carlton and Tianna ran into the room and hugged their father while Uncle Craig went to kiss his mother. "Hi, Grandma," Tianna was the first to speak.

"Hi, Grandma? You better get your butts over here and give your grandma a hug; both of you."

The two children happily ran over to their grandmother and into her arms. That's when Carl noticed that Jessica had walked in also. "Oh hi, Jessica. I'm sorry I didn't even see you."

"Me either, Sweetie. How are you? Come on in." Althea moved closer so that Jessica could reach her to kiss her on the cheek. "So, you guys kept my grandchildren last night, huh? How was it?"

"No, Craig kept them. I offered to come over to help out, but he said he could handle it." Jessica had been surprised when Craig turned down her help. She really didn't like kids but thought he would at least have wanted some adult companionship.

"Yeah, I promised to hang out with my niece and nephew, so that's what I did. Why do you guys act like it's a big deal? We had a great time. Right, kids?"

"Yeah, we had fun!" Tianna was full of excitement. "Uncle Craig said that we can stay over again too."

"So much for your theory," Althea said mockingly looking at Carl.

"What theory?" Craig asked while Jessica looked on very interested in what was being said.

"Mom and I were just joking about you having the kids." Carl gave his mother the *look*. "Neither of us could believe that they actually got you to spend a Saturday night with them."

"Instead of your woman," Althea blurted out before Craig could say anything. "I thought you two were over there playing house with my grandbabies, and you weren't even there. You must not be doing the right thing Ms. Jessi." Althea almost sung the last line.

Both Craig and Carl had to stop themselves from laughing at the way that Althea spoke and her candidness. They wondered where it was coming from.

"What, Mom?" After seeing the look on Jessica's face, Craig had to say something. "We just chilled out. I didn't want to bother Jessica because I know how she loves her weekends." He didn't know what else to say. The truth was that he wanted to bond with the kids, and he knew that with Jessica there, they would not have his undivided attention. They had never had a real conversation about children, but Craig got the feeling that Jessica didn't want any. "What are you trying to do to me?" He tried to make light of it.

"Bother her?" Althea sounded confused.

"I offered to come over." Jessica defended herself.

"Oh, I was just about to tell my son that he could go ahead and get rid of you, because any woman coming into this family had better love children." Althea added a little neck movement to the statement.

"Mom!" Craig said. "What has gotten into you? We don't even know what Jessica's plans are." He tried to flip the script. "Please excuse Mom, she just loves her grandbabies." He stretched his eyes when he looked at Jessica as a signal to show that their mother was totally out of character right now.

"Of course Jess likes children, Mother, but let's lay off that subject. We were talking about how Uncle Craig's night with your grandbabies went over without a glitch." Craig was shocked by his mother. He had no idea what her problem with Jessica was, but he tried to lighten the mood.

"Uncle Craig let us watch scary movies!" Tianna exclaimed. "Then Carlton was afraid to go to sleep." She added.

"He ain't no good." Grandma said. "Don't even know that babies don't need to be watching that kinda mess. Next time you go over there, I'm gonna come too since Ms. Jessi *loves* her weekends so much."

"Really, Grandma?" Carlton asked. "Is she really gonna stay?" He looked at Uncle Craig.

"We'll have to see about that." Craig winked and rustled Carlton's hair. "You know, it's my house and my rules and your Grandma doesn't like that."

"Don't worry baby. I'm *his* Momma."

Satisfied with their grandmother's answer, the two children ran to the back to see what they could find to play with.

CHAPTER THIRTY-THREE

"What time?" Zena asked Tia when she told her that Sean wanted them to meet him for drinks.

"In an hour. The place is on the water. You have somewhere you want to go before we go?"

"Aren't we going to change?" Zena was shocked because they hadn't stopped since the airport.

"No." Tia said sadly. "That is one of the things that I had to get use to with Sean. He is so spontaneous that I never know what to expect. I don't normally have the luxury of going home to shower and change to go out with him (as you know), so I basically have an emergency kit in the back." Tia grinned as if she had developed a new secret to success. "It contains a toothbrush, toothpaste, deodorant, some perfume, lotion and panties. I just make sure that I look hot when I leave the house and I can spruce up from my trunk if I need to." Tia realized that she sounded as if she was educating her friend on how to cheat on her husband.

"Are you serious?" Zena wasn't sure if Tia was joking about the panties. "You mean I have to go in your trunk, dig in my suitcase, pull out my necessities and go into a bathroom on the beach to get ready to meet this man?"

"You got it." Tia's smiled brightened knowing that her friend would do *whatever* for her. She had spruced up in quite a few public restrooms since her friendship with Sean began. However, she would choose the locations carefully. The Casino was one of her favorites because the restrooms were so nice and spacious, and they were always clean. It was also the perfect spot to be seen in for an alibi if she needed one. "Don't worry though, I won't make you go to the bathroom at the Shell station."

"I know you won't. Because Mr. Sean would just have to take it like it comes. What's his last name anyway?"

Zena's phone rang. "Hey." She barely let the phone ring before she answered. "Nope, we're still out and about. What's up with you?" She paused to listen to the response. "Okay, I will." She tried to contain the smile she felt coming through. "Bye."

Tia knew who was on the other end of that phone. The look on Zena's face after she hung up was the confirmation. Rick had an unbelievable effect over Zena and Tia thought that it should be a good thing, not something that Rick used like a tool to manipulate Zena. She was going to wait to see how far out of control it got before she stepped in. She knew that the sex was crazy between them, so she partially understood where her girl was coming from.

"I know he is not checking up on you already. You just got here, so you might as well go on and let him know that he might be a booty call. He'll probably love that anyway." Tia was snide but truthful. Carl already knew that it would be a late night for her since Z was just getting in. Tia had warned him that Zena might stay with them for at least one night. She didn't know what Sean's plans were, but they normally took advantage of any extra time they had to hang out together.

"Okay, T, don't hate. He just wanted to make sure that I call him whenever I got in." She saw Tia roll her eyes in disgust. "I'm telling you he has been on point with his shit lately. I'm looking for the slip, but he ain't slippin."

"Well, don't you slip. And you know I ain't hatin on you, I just don't want you to get set up"…*(Again)*. Tia thought it but decided not to add the last word.

"Okay, I know, Tia. Now, where are we going so I can put on some lip gloss, pee, and tighten up?"

"This is Sean we're going to see, not Rick. You're tightening up for the wrong brother." Tia said with a smirk. She knew what Zena meant because they had stopped to get some conch salad earlier, so she wanted to brush her teeth and freshen up herself. Tia didn't remember checking, but she was sure that Rosina had smudged something when she tweezed the tough strands that couldn't be captured by the thread when they got their eyebrows done. She would lightly reapply her makeup, but she didn't want to look as though she had gotten perfect just for Sean, although she did have him in mind when she chose the short, silk, grey dress that was loose and flowing just right and the strappy sandals that she wore.

Zena was digging in her purse to see if she could make do with what she had or if she really had to go into her suitcase. "I'm getting butterflies like he's my date. I guess because my expectations are so high now, I'm expecting some charming ass Denzel Washington type and I just want to be on point. Okay, Honey?" Zena looked at Tia slyly out of the corner of her eye. "You want it to be love at first sight, right?"

"Don't play." The words came out before Tia really thought about what she was saying.

The two must have had the same thought at the same time, but Zena said it first. "You two are just friends, right?"

"You know what? Don't even go there."

For the first time since Zena had gotten in with Tia, the car was silent.

Tia pulled up alongside of the W Hotel. She put the car in park and turned to her friend. "Do you know that I have never even thought about it that way? If Sean and I were *really* just friends, I would have already tried to hook you two up. You know that."

"Honestly, T, I hadn't even broken it down that way before myself. I could hear in your voice that it was a little more than the *just friends* that you try to make it." Zena grabbed her purse. "Let's go girl. No sense in stressing now, especially since I want to meet him to see just how irresistible he really is."

The thought of Sean's irresistibility pepped Tia up again. She smiled and reached for her bag from the backseat. They laughed their way into The W and Zena was shocked by the vibe. "Oh, I forgot that you hadn't been here before. It just opened a couple of months ago. I think it's beautiful. This would be our spot for drinks if your ass didn't live across the country." Tia could not let that opportunity to drop a hint pass. "Let's have one anyway. I want to check the bar out."

Zena was busy checking the place out. She was looking for a check in desk, but there wasn't one in sight. They had walked into a huge open space with large sofas, chairs, and lounges on either side, sitting on artsy area rugs that were placed on top of the marble floor. The lounge had sheer curtains on the posts that could be spread out to provide privacy. There were tables strategically placed throughout holding books and trendy magazines. Two teenagers were sitting in a circular chair with a laptop between them, oblivious to what was going on around them. Three men were seated together, talking. There was a woman in a secluded corner of the lobby reading a newspaper. "You're right. I like this, there was never anyplace this nice when I lived here. Where is the bar?"

"I'm not sure. Let's check the place out, we'll find it."

The two took an elevator to the second floor where Zena noticed the check in desk. They kept going to the third floor. When they heard a sultry voice singing *You Belong to Me,* they knew they were going in the right direction. The bar looked just as contemporary as the lobby had and there were quite a few people standing around drinking and talking. Tia and Zena both ordered martinis.

They got their drinks and grabbed a seat at the bar. Zena took a sip and then a gulp. The deejay was playing a new hit and Zena got lost in her thoughts. "You know I cannot forget about Rick's ass." She said before she put her martini glass back to her lips.

Tia laughed. "That was the plan, Crazy. He wants you to keep thinking about him showing up at the airport smelling good and looking better. He knows that we are probably somewhere getting tipsy, so he expects you to hit him with the booty call."

They crack up laughing. "After a couple of these, he just might get it." Zena raised her glass in the air. She was enjoying herself, Tia, and the ambiance. She missed the comforts of being home. She missed her best friend and being able to hang out with someone that really knew her and how to have a good time. "This drink is delicious, but it is strong."

"I know. Look. Mine is gone already. I want another, but I want to be able to keep my composure when we get to

Sean. I already feel like I might rip his clothes off when I see him." Tia was feeling the effects of the first martini.

"You are silly." Zena giggled. "Please refrain yourself. At least let me get to know the guy first. I don't know if it's these drinks or this place and all the sexy undertones, but Rick is on the brain."

"You mean dick is on the brain. Let's get out of here. This whole setup is an aphrodisiac."

The two of them walked to the elevator feeling buzzed and laughing at the way they easily slipped back into their old ways. There was a very well-dressed white man on the elevator when Tia and Zena got in. "Looks like the two of you have started the evening off nicely. Where's the party?" He asked, although he looked like he knew just where to go.

"You should tell us." Tia quickly responded.

"As beautiful as the two of you look, I'm sure your night will be better than mine. I'm meeting some friends over at Jackson's. Have you eaten? Their food is the best." He casually spoke as he stood aside to let the ladies exit.

"Actually, we're meeting someone for dinner ourselves, but thank you for the invitation." That time Zena answered as she admired the handsome stranger with the carefree attitude.

"Yes, I've heard good things about that place. We should go before you leave." Tia said to Zena. "It's always packed when I go by there." She said to them both as they walked out into the open air.

"Business is good." He said with a smile. "So, you're here visiting? Your friend here must be showing you around." He looked directly at Zena when he spoke.

"Yes. Nice talking to you." Zena said as they approached their turn to the car.

"By the way I'm John; John Steiner." He said as he extended his hand to Zena. "Didn't you valet?"

"No. We just stopped by for a drink, so we parked in front. I'm Tia; Tia

Lawson, and this is my friend Zena."

Tia answered before realizing that Mr. Steiner seemed to be speaking directly to Z.

"It's a pleasure." He answered quickly. "Did you say Tina?"

"Zena, with a Z."

"Beautiful name, Zena. Please," he paused while he went into the inside pocket of his sports jacket, "take my card. If you have time while you're here, I would love to take the two of you to dinner." He looked at them both. "I'll be in town until next week."

Zena took his card and briefly looked it over. "Well, thank you for the offer. We'll give you a call."

"I look forward to it. You ladies have a wonderful evening."

"You too." Zena replied, and she and Tia headed towards the car.

CHAPTER THIRTY-FOUR

Z ena thought the spot they just left was nice, and from pulling up outside of the place where they were meeting Sean, she could tell that this would be another treat. The parking lot was lined with expensive foreign cars and Tia had barely stopped the car before both doors were opened simultaneously by the valets. When she stepped out of the car, Zena could see that the two-story restaurant had a 360-degree view, she could see straight through to the beach where there were different sized cabanas for private outdoor dining. "Wow, this place looks nice," Zena said to Tia who was looking in her Chanel bag for her phone.

"Don't call yet," Zena said, "I want to go to the ladies' room first."

"Good idea," Tia replied and closed her purse. They walked in and Tia said, "We're meeting someone, but can you tell us where the ladies' room is?" She was speaking to the hostess that had rushed to open the door for them and welcome them in. Tia seemed unimpressed with the opulence of the place. Once inside the ladies' room, they both went to the mirror to make sure that they looked the part. "I hope he didn't see us walk in." Tia said while she seemed to take extra care to make sure that her figure was looking right in the dress that she was wearing.

They both already knew that they looked great. "Ok. Let's do it." Zena said after she finished perfecting her hair. "I am ready to meet Sean. What's his last name?" Tia's phone rang as Zena headed for the door.

"That's probably him."

"Hi." Tia answered her phone while nodding her head up and down at Zena. "We'll be there in a sec." She smiled into the phone. "I guess I can't get anything past you. Zena needed to stop by the ladies' room,"

Tia winked at her friend. "But we'll be right up."

Tia ended the call and leaned her back up against the wall for support. Zena saw the distant look in Tia's eyes and the soft smile on her lips and she mentally prepared herself for the coming event. Tia had always been a tough cookie to break. For her to be shook, let Zena know that this Sean guy was a smooth operator. "Can you get it together so we can get out of here?" Zena tugged Tia's arm bringing her back to reality. She gave Tia a squeeze with one arm and the two of them walked out.

They walked through the beautiful restaurant toward a spiral staircase and could feel the eyes follow them as they passed table after table of couples and groups. They got to the top of the staircase and Tia heard Sean's familiar voice. "Well, hello." He reached for her hand and kissed her on the cheek, helping her up the final stair. Once Tia was secure and Sean had drunk in as much of her as he could drink with his eyes, he reached for Zena's hand. "Zena," Sean said with a toothy smile. "Nice to finally meet you." He kissed her on the cheek also.

'Nice to meet you too, Sean." Zena could see, immediately, what got Tia's panties in a bunch. For Zena, the atmosphere of the place, alone, was a turn on. The upstairs dining area was more intimate than downstairs and the mood more relaxed. There were fewer tables, and they were all strategically set around the circular bar which was in the middle of the large area. The rich sound of contemporary jazz engulfed the room, so people had to lean in close to speak to each other. Zena didn't remember hearing music downstairs. She hoped that she could stay composed, but she felt intoxicated by Sean's cologne. She never met a man that smelled so good in her life. Sean was not drop dead gorgeous or not even overly handsome, but very polished and masculine with gorgeous, smooth, dark skin and very white teeth making him a treat for Zena's eyes.

"Our table is ready if the two of you are." Sean said smoothly.

Tia smiled and looked at Z who was still trying to take everything in. "Show us the way." She said and looped her arm through Zena's. Sean led them to one of the few tables for four. Most of the tables were small and intimate; set for two.

Zena leaned into her friend's ear and whispered. "I'm in love." The two of them snuck in a giggle before Sean stopped to pull out Zena's chair.

The waiter came from nowhere and gently put his hand on Sean's back to let him know that he was there. Sean stood and waited for both ladies to be seated.

Once they were all seated with their menus and the waiter excused himself, Sean smiled at both ladies. "So, what are we drinking ladies?" he asked. "Champagne?" he looked at Zena, then Tia.

When neither of them answered, Sean looked at Tia and asked, "What are you in the mood for, Babe?"

Zena was dazed by the way Sean spoke to Tia. It was strange to hear someone that she didn't know speak so affectionately to her best friend.

Tia was looking at Z for some help. Zena felt that it was a perfect time to "turn up" but didn't know how Tia would feel in front of Sean so she didn't make the call. "I'm a guest and I don't know how you guys do it, so one of you will have to choose the poison."

"I think it would be nice to pop a bottle of champagne. You up for it?" Sean smiled then reached over and gave Tia's leg a squeeze beneath the table.

"Let's do it." Tia flashed a bright smile towards Sean. She could not contain her pleasure to be spending time with Zena *and* Sean.

Sean waved the waiter over and ordered a bottle of Imperial Rose. "Ok, I have to make sure that you ladies eat because I won't be able to carry the both of you out of here. The food is great here." He glossed over the menu and said, "I'm having the lamb chops. They're my favorite."

The waiter returned with the bubbly and Sean placed everyone's order. After that, Sean decided to dig in and get some information. "So, the two of you are lifelong BFF's." He smiled in Zena's direction.

"Fa life!" Tia said.

"Yep. She's stuck with me." Zena replied taking a better look at Sean.

"So, you're the person who knows all of her dirt, huh?" Sean was speaking to Zena but smiling at Tia.

"Dirt? I keep telling you that I don't have any of that. Why won't you believe me?"

"He must have heard about the tell all novel that I just finished." Zena added jokingly.

The three of them laughed and talked over a delicious meal.

"Zena, what do you do over there on the other side of the world?"

"I must say that I am not doing what you guys are doing over here." She smiled. "I mean everything here is so grand. I haven't had the chance to get out much there, but I'm pretty sure that it doesn't compare." She hoped Sean *or* Tia (for that matter) didn't think that she meant *them* when she said, "not what you guys are doing". There was really no shade intended. "I moved because of a job offer *and* a need to get away." Zena added the last part as an afterthought and Rick flashed across her mind. "I think the move has just about served its purpose, so I don't know how long I'm going to be 'on the other side of the world', as you put it." She smiled at Tia whose face lit up at her words.

"Yeah, she keeps teasing me with the thought of her moving back." Tia pretended to be over it.

"It's not me." Zena squealed, already affected by the bubbly. "These things take time and are never final until they're final, so I don't want to get my hopes up." Zena said honestly.

"Which is why I haven't even mentioned it to anyone because I don't want to get my hopes up either." Tia admitted.

"Well, you just read my mind, Tia. I was wondering why you wouldn't have shared such good news with me." Sean's voice was genuine. "So, that gives us more reason to celebrate. A toast to more nights like this." Sean poured the last of the champagne into the 3 flutes and they raised them.

"You're gonna have to bring some friends if this is how we're doing it." Zena laughed but she was serious.

"That's not a problem." Sean said as their glasses clinked. "What do you plan on doing once you're back?"

That led to a different conversation because Zena was waiting to get some news on a job that she had been interviewing for. It was a great position as superintendent of the 5th largest school district in the country, but Zena knew that it would be a lot of work. She also knew that it was just another JOB and not what she genuinely wanted to do forever. Zena's hope was to use the position as the vehicle to get her back to her hometown. She didn't know if Tia remembered or was ever even serious all those years ago about the two of them going into business.

They finished the drinks and walked outside. It was a beautiful night, and the strip was alive.

"That was the best meal that I've had in a long time." Zena seemed to have taken control of her buzz.

"Yes, everything was delicious." Tia chimed in, looking at Sean.

"Glad you ladies enjoyed it."

"I've never been over here. When did they do all of this?

"The area was here, but most of the original owners were bought out by some young investors with a great vision." Sean responded to Zena.

"I enjoy the atmosphere more every time I'm over here."

"Is that a live band that I hear?" Tia wasn't ready to leave. She didn't know the area either and she wanted to explore.

"It sounds like it. Wanna check it out?" Sean wasn't ready to leave either. He hoped the ladies were interested. He was enjoying the evening and felt amazingly comfortable and carefree with Tia and Zena. Sean couldn't remember the last time that he felt so at ease besides when he was alone with Tia. It may have been the alcohol, but Sean thought it was the company that he was in.

"I want to. I'm sorry. I know I'm the third wheel tonight, but I'm not ready to leave." Zena admitted it hoping she didn't sound pitiful. Although Sean was so warm and welcoming that Zena really did not feel like an intruder. It felt like she was out with two friends.

"I want to see who they are. They sound great from here." The three of them began walking in the direction of the music. "Portuguese Love! I haven't heard that in years." Tia felt the need to walk faster, as if that was the band's last song.

"If I didn't know better, I would say that was Tina herself."

The crowd began to get thicker before the threesome got to Ginger's Bay, where the band was playing. Ginger's was packed and Sean realized why. There was a banner promoting a local band Everything and a Dream…Friday, Saturday and Sunday nights. Sean had heard a lot about Everything and a Dream but had never heard them play.

"Rick has mentioned this band before." Zena said to Tia. "I wonder if he knows they're playing here."

"If he doesn't, I'm sure he will." Tia answered with feigned sarcasm. Since Zena had been open to meeting Sean, Tia knew that she should probably lighten up on Rick.

"Rick, huh?" Sean didn't miss anything. "Why didn't you bring him along?"

Tia's facial expression answered the question for Zena, but she didn't say a word.

"I wanted to meet you tonight Sean, since I've heard so much about you. Rick and I are just friends, but his presence would have added a different dynamic to the evening."

"I'll say." Tia added a bit of sarcasm while swaying to the music.

"You ladies up for a glass of wine? I don't think they have champagne here…but they might." Sean added because he didn't want to underestimate the place.

"Wine is fine." Tia answered for them both.

Sean walked inside to try to make his way to the bar and Zena took advantage of the opportunity. "He is amazing! I have been waiting for the bullshit to begin, but he seems genuine. What are you going to do with him?" Zena was serious. Her friend was in a bad position; married to a great and loving husband while being courted by this nice, friendly, sexy ass being.

They laughed at the dilemma that was on Tia's mind constantly. Before long, they could both see Sean's masculinity making his way back over to them. He arrived with 3 wine glasses, a bottle of Pinot and a smile directed at Tia. When Zena saw the way the two of them looked at each other, she was glad that she was the third wheel. If the two of them were out on that beautiful night alone, with the band now playing Kenny G's version of "I Like the Way You Move", and the Pinot Grigio flowing, she didn't think that the night would have ended without bodily fluids being exchanged.

They laughed and talked some more while they finished the bottle of wine. A couple visiting from Canada came over and started talking with them. They even danced a little, and

Zena could see why Rick liked the band. They were great at keeping the crowd engaged, they looked nice, and their sound was fantastic. The night was over when the band finished their last set. Tia could not believe it was 3:00 AM.

They walked back to the restaurant where the cars were parked to find both cars at the front and one lone valet waiting. They apologized profusely. Sean compensated him nicely and they got into their cars. Sean felt that he needed to follow them, but Tia assured him that she was fine and could drive home with no problem.

Zena could not wait to have Tia to herself. "Oh my God, Girl, what are you going to do?" Zena almost screamed at her friend when they pulled off. "I see why you could not stop talking to him, and the way he looks at you is intoxicating!!!" Although Zena loved Carl and always wished the best for her best friend's marriage, she could not help but feel some level of excitement for this new "friendship" that Tia found. "Poor Carl." Zena spoke subconsciously.

"Poor Carl? Really Z? Please do not make me feel any worse than I already feel." Tia looked at her friend and Zena thought that she saw a tear glistening, on the verge of falling out of Tia's eyes.

"I'm sorry, but you know I love Carl and I just think he's up against something big right now. That's all I'm saying, T." Zena paused for a moment to gather her thoughts. "I don't know what's going on or what you're feeling. All I know is that Sean looks at you like you are the only woman on earth, he speaks to you like you are a queen and you have been walking around in a daze since we met up with him. I haven't seen you act this way since...NEVER. You have never been the starry-eyed girl, in love who can't think straight, and you know it yourself. No matter who you've dated, how fine they were, what their status was, how much money they threw, you always seemed to be in control."

"I'm in control. So, you're saying that I'm not in control right now? "Tia already knew the answer. She just didn't know that it was obvious.

"T, I'm only saying that I have never seen you behave this way. I am not saying that there is anything wrong with it. I wish I could go brain-dead and have someone like Sean to lead me around." Zena leaned her head back against the headrest. "I don't know. I need to sleep on this one. My head is all over the place and it wasn't even my date, so I can only imagine how you must be feeling."

"It was not a date."

"Oh yeah, I forgot. What was it again?" Zena smirked.

"Shut up. It was a meeting." Tia couldn't help but join Zena in laughter.

"There's going to be a meeting at your house that may not turn out to be so much fun if you turn this corner with Sean following us." Zena was very matter of fact.

"Oh my goodness, I forgot." Tia was frantically digging for her phone. She pulled it from the bottom of her purse and pressed his name. She didn't even want to look over at Zena who was shaking her head. "Hey, you didn't have to follow us all the way over here. I hope you aren't too far from home." Tia smiled while she spoke. "Now we may need to follow you."

Zena thought about calling Rick while Tia spoke to Sean. When she heard the conversation ending, she decided not to make the call.

"Thank you again and drive safely. I'm gonna wait for your call." She pressed end. "Girl, do you see why you have to come home? I was not thinking."

"I know, Miss 'In Control'." They laughed as Tia pulled into her circular driveway.

Chapter Thirty-Five

Tia struggled to open her eyes. She had been awakened by the soft kiss that Carl placed on her lips, but her body was not ready to move. She had only gone to sleep a couple hours before Carl walked into the den. He was looking right into Tia's eyes when she finally got them to open. "I missed you last night." Carl said before he placed another gentle kiss on Tia's lips.

"Mmmmmm." That was the only sound that Tia could manage as she repositioned herself on the comfortable sofa where she had fallen asleep.

Carl sat there, on the side of the sofa and absorbed the sight of Tia. He wondered if he should make coffee. Tia looked beautifully exhausted, and Zena was on the sofa across from her just...passed out. He needed to warn the two of them that "The Nerds" would be coming by soon. When Dominique called last night, Carl should have known not to mention the fact that Zena was in town. As soon as Carl said that Tia was out with Zena, Dominique shouted it out to his wife. "Hey Jan, Z's in town."

Carl walked into the kitchen and decided to make a pot of the Blue Mountain coffee that Tia had recently brought home from somewhere. After seeing them stretched out in there, Carl knew that Tia and Zena would probably knock a pot of coffee off before they even showered; especially when they found out about Nique and Jan coming through.

"Hi, Carl." Zena was struggling to smile. "I'm sorry that you had to find me like this." Her face was partially covered by the comforter that she slept under.

"Come on Z, I knew you would be somewhere around here. I don't know why your girl put you on the couch though."

"Zena knows where her room is. We just fell asleep down here." Tia spoke through her grogginess.

"Good morning, Baby." Carl smiled lovingly at Tia. "The coffee should be ready in a few."

"Good."

"Yeah, you're gonna need it." Carl paused. "I told Nique that Zena was here, so you already know they wanna come through."

"Oh my goodness, I didn't tell Z." Tia looked at Zena who only had one eye open. "Jan's having a baby."

"Good, maybe her and her husband will get a life." Zena shot. Carl laughed from the kitchen. "Go easy, Z. They're excited about the baby. They haven't realized that no one else really cares."

"Well, it's about time for a wakeup call. How long on the coffee?" Zena sat up. "Knowing those two, they will be ringing the doorbell any minute now. And I at least want a cup of coffee before seeing 'The Nerds'".

"I think I may need more than that to deal with them. You haven't heard the kicker, Z. We are the Godparents."

Zena burst out laughing. "Girl, you are crazy! You will be watching the little nerdy baby by yourself, and please do not force the little nerd on my niece and nephew." She couldn't stop laughing at the thought of Zena parenting for Nique and Janice. "You two are the best friends that they have?"

"How should I take that?" Carl asked coming from the kitchen with two cups of coffee and condiments on a silver tray.

"No, Carl, it's not you. It's Tia, and the way she treats them is shady and you know it." Zena reached for her cup. "Thanks. This is so nice." "And much needed." Tia added. "Thank you, Baby." She sat up and appreciated her husband. "Don't listen to the haters." She whispered loudly and met his lips with a kiss.

The doorbell rang and the three of them burst into laughter.

Rick's timing was perfect. No sooner had Zena taken care of the hugs and air kisses did she hear her phone ring.

"Oh, I have to take this." Zena said when she looked and saw that it was Rick calling. She walked into the guest bedroom where she usually slept when visiting. "Good morning." She answered.

"Good morning." Rick paused. "What's up? I didn't really expect you to be up."

"Trust me, I didn't expect to be up myself. But you know how it is…when in Rome. What are you up to?"

"I'm tryin' to get with you. That's why I'm calling so early. I wanted to be first in line."

Zena smiled. "What did you have in mind?"

"How about, I come pick you up and we figure the rest out after that?"

Rick's cool confidence was still a turn on to Zena. She quickly thought about what she had packed. "How long before you get here?" She was eager to rock the one shouldered jumpsuit that she had with her. It was sexy and casual but could easily go from day to night if needed.

"I can be there in thirty. Have you had breakfast?" Rick was already dressed and ready to go.

"Nope, I still don't eat breakfast, but come on. I'll see you when you get here."

"Okay."

"Leave now, Ricky." Zena teased. She could hear it in Rick's voice that he wanted to see her, and she knew that he would be there in thirty minutes or less.

She hung up the phone and went to get her things. She had no plans on wasting precious time on Jan and Dom.

When Zena got out of the shower, she could hear Tianna and Carlton running around. She wanted to spend some time with them, but Rick and his offer were sounding too good to pass up. As Zena continued to get dressed, she got more and more excited about seeing Rick. It felt like old times. When they were dating, Zena and Rick always had a good time together. That's why she couldn't understand how he could mess it up the way that he did.

The two quick knocks on the door startled Zena and was followed by Tia entering. "What the hell?" Tia faked surprise when she saw Z in the mirror putting on makeup. "I know you aren't tryin' to escape."

"I can't take it, T. Remember that I'm on vacation, but I'm prayin' for you." She couldn't see Tia's face because she was looking at her own.

"You probably need some rest from that turn up last night anyway."

Tia blushed at the thought.

"Rick called. He's on his way. I'll be back to chill with my niece and nephew."

"When did you start doing breakfast?" Tia asked seriously.

"I don't, he said he was just trying to catch me early."

"That's cute." Tia said before they heard the doorbell ring. "Nique and Carl are going to hit a couple balls on the golf course. What am I going to do with Jan's boring ass?"

"Really, T? I am so sorry, but when Rick called, I guess I went into a time warp. I didn't even consider saying 'no'. You know I would not have left you like this if I knew that they were going to leave you here with her." Zena really sympathized with her friend. They say when you marry someone, you marry their friends also. Well, Carl's friends suck.

She quickly slipped the jumpsuit on and pulled the shoes out of her suitcase. Zena thought flat sandals would look nice since she didn't really know where they were going. She thought heels would make her look like she was trying too hard. She put the shoes on and turned to walk over to the mirror, but the look on Tia's face told Zena everything she needed to know.

"Oh, you can leave that outfit *and* the shoes when you leave." Tia's eyes were gleaming at Zena who was looking fresh and pretty. "I know you only bought it for Rick's ass anyway."

Zena looked in the mirror and was pleased. "I've had it for a minute, but this is my first time wearing it."

"Like I said…" Tia was in the middle of her sentence when Zena grabbed her purse and the two of them walked out of the room.

Tia elbowed Z as they heard Rick congratulating "The Nerds" on their pregnancy. They both rolled their eyes to the top of their heads. "Please tell me that I did not think that the whole world was excited when I got pregnant."

"No, but you hadn't been trying forever either."

"Hey." Rick greeted Zena with a full-blown smile and a kiss on the lips.

"Wow, you clean up nice." Carl said.

"Don't act like you don't know me, Carl."

"You both look nice." Jan added. "I didn't know you two got back together."

Zena just ignored Jan. "I'm ready when you are." She spoke softly to Rick. He was wearing jeans and a T shirt, but looked delicious. Zena wanted to get out of the crowd so she could tell him how nice he looked for a Saturday morning.

"Auntie Z!" Carlton yelled.

"Hi, Auntie." Tianna's squeaky voice sounded so cute as the twins ran into the room and hugged Zena. "Mommy said you were staying with us." She said it as if it were a question.

"I am, Baby Girl. We got in late, and your mommy wouldn't let me wake you guys." Zena bent to give both the kids a hug and noticed that Carlton had gotten quite a bit taller than Tianna. She moved back a step to hold him at arm's length with her hands on his shoulders. "When did you get so tall, Carlton?" Tears came to her eyes as she realized that the kids were really growing up.

"I don't know." Carlton looked at Carl for an answer.

Tianna's hair had grown down her back and was in one big wild ponytail. Zena remembered when she and Tia worried that Tianna would be bald. Her hair didn't grow at all until she was about 3 years old. Zena kissed Tianna on the top of her head. "I see your mom still hasn't learned how to do hair."

"Nope, I do my own hair." Tianna answered proudly.

"Well maybe you and I will go to the spa, and we can get our hair done before I leave."

"Coo-ool." Tianna made the word two syllables.

"What about me, Auntie Z?"

"Well, I'm sure we can find something 'cool' to do too; probably before

Tianna and I get our hair done."

"Can I come too?"

"That won't be fair, T. Unless Carlton comes to the spa with us."

"No way!" The twins spoke in unison.

"We'll see. We'll find a way to all have fun. I miss you guys so much." She hugged them one more time. Zena was really shocked at how much the two of them had changed. It had only been six months since she had seen them last.

Tia enjoyed seeing Zena with the kids. She was really the sister that Tia never had, and Tia knew that Z absolutely loved the twins. She was just as excited as her and Carl through their whole pregnancy. She went to Lamaze classes with them and didn't mind being a third wheel. Zena met them at the hospital for the delivery but couldn't stomach being in the delivery room. She said best friends or not, she had to draw the line somewhere. Tianna and Carlton were giving Z a list of 'fun' things they could do when Tia remembered that Rick was waiting. "Guys, Auntie Z will be back. Can you let her go before she gets left?" Tia knew that Rick wouldn't leave. She saw his eyes sparkle as soon as he looked at Zena. Tia couldn't understand why it took men so long to realize when they have a good woman on their team.

Rick had joined the conversation with Zena and the twins and was telling Carlton that they could go shoot some ball while Tianna and Zena had their spa day.

"When? When?" Carlton was impatient.

"We're gonna have to work on the details, Sweeties. I'm only gonna be here for a few days."

"Tell your auntie that she needs to move home." Carl said jokingly.

"Not you too." She rolled her eyes in Carl's direction. "I'm working on it. Then you guys can come and stay with me." Zena didn't like to talk about it, but she really wanted to be at home with her friends and her family.

Carl noticed the surprise look on Rick's face and wondered what was going on. "Alright, kids, she's gotta go. Auntie Z will be back. Her things are in the room. Go look." He knew how to divert their attention.

"I should have come a day earlier just for them. I feel negligent by leaving when I haven't done anything with them yet." Then Zena remembered that she bought them both AirPods. She ran into the room to dig them out of her suitcase.

"Sssshhhh. Don't let Mommy and Daddy see until I'm gone, ok?" She knew that new gadgets would keep them occupied for a while.

Zena left the room unnoticed by the two kids. She entered the kitchen and heard Jan saying to T that she was surprised that the children were so attached to me. "Well, that's normally how it is with aunties; especially when you live in another state and bring gifts and good times whenever you visit." Zena knew that was not the only reason that the kids loved her. She was their auntie as far as the twins were concerned, and the love went both ways. Zena couldn't imagine not being a part of their lives.

"Yeah, it doesn't hurt that she showers them with gifts." Carl chuckled although he knew that his kids loved Zena dearly.

"You ready?" Zena asked Rick.

"Whenever you are."

"It was nice seeing you guys. Congrats again on the baby."

"Thanks." Nique replied.

"When are you leaving?" Janice asked.

"I'm supposed to leave Wednesday." Zena answered walking towards the door. "See you later, T." She said sympathetically. "Have fun." She winked at Tia as she and Rick walked out the door.

CHAPTER THIRTY-SIX

Rick was glad to finally have Zena to himself. He had been dreaming about this day for a while and wasn't sure that he would ever get the opportunity. He realized that he really messed up by cheating on Zena and he regretted it.

Rick dated quite a few women since the breakup, but none of them meant anything to him. Even with Eva, the one that Zena caught him cheating with, there was nothing there. Eva was basically a showpiece, and it took losing Zena for Rick to find out that he didn't want to spend his life with someone who was just arm candy. Zena was beautiful and sexy. She was also smart and funny and on top all of that, RicKenjoyed being with her and he had been spending a lot of time thinking of ways to get Zena back. He had already decided that he would relocate if it came down to that.

Rick went to open the door for Zena and caught a whiff of the scent that she had worn for years. It was the most beautiful and feminine scent, and he couldn't understand why he never smelled it on anyone else. He remembered the first time she spent the weekend at his place. His bathroom smelled of her for days.

He got in, started the car and buckled up. "You're all mine now. You ready to hang?"

"You know I stay ready." Zena smiled. "Where're we off to?"

"They're having an open house over at The Acreage."

"They've finished it?" Zena loved that area. She was the one that had taken Rick by there for the first time. They used to drive through all the time and watch the progress being made. They both thought it would be one of the most desired places to live for those that could afford it. The last time that Zena went there with Rick, the land had just been cleared and the foundation was laid for a couple of the homes.

"Today's the first showing. It'll probably be packed, although the

project won't be complete until the end of the year."

"I can't wait to see what they've done."

"Good, I was hoping you were up for it. I thought it ironic that the open house is on the weekend that you're in town and now, we just *happen* to be going to check it out together."

"You think it's a sign?" Zena teased. "I'm the one that turned you on to the area anyway. Hell, we should have designed the place as many times as we drove through there fantasizing."

"Fa real." He laughed before his voice became serious. "I always imagined us moving into a house over there."

"So did I." Zena admitted and sat back in her seat getting comfortable for the ride.

They rode the rest of the way without talking. Rick had a playlist full of Zena's favorite artists. They each quietly enjoyed the music, the ride, and the ease of each other's company.

"Oh my goodness." It was as if the whisper escaped from Zena's mouth.

Rick was so deep in thought that her voice startled him. "Wow, this is beautiful."

They were just driving through the iron arches that read "The Acreage" in sculpted letters atop the arch. The landscape at the entry was beautiful and the colorful flowers left a bright path for Rick to follow to the welcome center.

The welcome center was set up beautifully. The smell of fresh baked cookies and bright smiling faces greeted them as soon as they opened the door to walk in. "Welcome home." A young blonde handed them both brochures that were more like magazines as they entered the building. "Have a seat and take a look at the floor plans. Denise will be here to answer your questions and give you a tour in just a few moments."

They sat on the comfortable leather sectional next to another couple. Zena couldn't take her eyes off the house on the front of the brochure while Rick was already turning pages.

"Can I offer any of you a drink? We have coffee, tea and water." A pretty, young girl came up with a tray of warm chocolate chip cookies to tempt the guests. It seemed as if no one could turn down a warm cookie.

"May I have water?" Rick and the gentleman next to him responded in unison.

"Anything for you ladies?"

"I'll have tea, please." The other woman responded.

"No, thank you." Zena answered while trying to find the floor plan of the house on the cover.

"Looks like she's found what she likes." The older gentleman spoke to Rick. "Hold on to your wallet." He joked.

Zena smiled politely. That's when she finally made eye contact with the man sitting next to Rick. He was fine. He and the woman that he was with were an extremely attractive couple and well-dressed too.

"We're just looking today." Rick responded respectfully.

"It's nice to see young folk like you making these kinds of investments."

"It's nice that they can *afford* these types of investments." The woman spoke softly.

"Well, that's yet to be seen. We haven't heard any numbers yet." He winked at the gentleman. Rick was making casual conversation, but he had always been a saver and his credit was excellent. He was confident that he would be able to swing it.

"You look like a smart young man. I bet you've been making good investments for a while." The gentlemen responded.

Rick liked the sound of that and wondered how the man was so intuitive.

"You don't get to be with women like these by squandering finances."

The two men chuckled as the older gentleman stood. He reached for Rick's hand with one of his and with the other, he gave him an encouraging pat on the shoulder. "What's your name?"

"Richard; Richard Townsend," Rick answered, standing. "This is
Zena."

"Well, it's very nice to meet the two of you. We're the Franklin's and we wish you the best." He put his hand out for his wife to hold on to. "I think I saw the car come around."

The woman took his hand and stood. She rubbed Zena's shoulder in a motherly fashion. "Nice to meet you, Zena. That's a beautiful name."

"I think we'll see them again." Mr. Franklin smiled. "Let's go, Dear."

The well-dressed couple walked out and walked towards a black Mercedes with tinted windows. That's when a gorgeous exotic woman came over and handed her well-manicured hand to Rick. "Mr. Townsend?"

"Yes, and this is Zena."

"I'm Anicka, and I will be showing your home today. Did you have your eye on any one in particular or would you like to see all of the six models?"

Rick looked at Zena. "Can we start with your largest home and work our way down?"

"Whatever you like Mr. Townsend."

Zena smiled. This contractor was laying it on thick with the beautiful women, making googlie eyes at the men, the plush welcome center and even the cookies. She knew that the price was going to be crazy, but she enjoyed looking at beautiful homes even if she wasn't buying.

"Follow me." Anicka showed the couple to the back of the welcome center and over to a golf cart. "I like the way you think, Mr. Townsend. I think it's a great idea to start with the biggest and the baddest and there may be no need to even see all the models." She winked at Zena and smiled.

"Well, no matter what happens I want to at least see the inside of the one that's unsurpassed. If I end up in one of the other ones, I won't have to wonder what the inside of the 'Mountainview' looks like."

They all laughed as Anicka drove and they scanned the property with all its majesty. The 'Mountainview' was the largest home on the property and the model stood out against the rest. It was the farthest away, but they could see it clearly, and it commanded attention as they rode through the grounds.

CHAPTER THIRTY-SEVEN

Jessica was the first to notice the gentleman walking towards Althea's house and approaching the front door. She didn't know who it was, but she hoped that it was some type of doctor coming to find out what the hell was wrong with the woman. She was about two seconds from being told off. It would have been done already, but she wasn't ready to let Craig see that side of her yet, especially by unleashing on his mother.

Everyone looked when the doorbell rang, and Craig got up. "I got it." Althea spoke defensively.

"No problem, Mom. Who is it?" Craig asked as gently as possible. He had already seen the man at the door and wondered who he was.

Carl wondered if that was the friend that his mother said was stopping by. "Oh, you were serious about having company?" He was speaking to his mother but shot a puzzled look at his brother.

"Well, hello." Althea opened the door as she spoke. "Come on in. My two sons are here."

The man walked in and kissed Althea on the cheek. "I finally get to meet them. I was starting to wonder if they even existed."

"This is Carl, and this is Craig. That's Craig's friend Jessica. This is one of my church friends, Adam Tillman. They were just about to leave when you came up." Althea dropped the hint hard. She had forgotten about her two grandchildren in the back who came running out once they heard a new voice in the room.

"This is your church friend, Grandma?" Tianna asked.

"So, here's Tianna and Carlton. Today must be my lucky day."

"Yes, I'm Tianna."

"I'm Carlton."

"Go get your things." Carl told the children, still puzzled by his mother's bluntness and the fact that Mr. Tillman knew more than he expected about their family.

Althea walked to the back of the house with the twins to collect their things.

"It's nice to meet you Mr. Tillman." Craig shook the man's hand.

"I'm going to have to get by the church more often." Carl added as he extended his hand.

"It's always nice to have a new face in the house of The Lord." Mr. Tillman responded with a tightly gripped handshake. "I think Thea wanted to keep you two hidden. I've asked a couple of times when I would have the pleasure of meeting the men in her life.

"Wow." Craig could not contain himself. "Really?" He was looking at Carl. "She's never mentioned it to me."

"Your daddy may bring you by tomorrow if you're a good girl." Althea was escorting Tianna to the front of the house.

"Mr. Tillman said that he's been asking to meet us, Mom."

"Adam, I told you that these boys are busy. They only come over here, to use my basement for their business and to eat."

"If you had mentioned Mr. Tillman to us, you know that we would have made time, Mother." Carl responded truthfully and Althea knew it. "Do you golf? Maybe we can hit some balls one day."

"Bye, Carl, get these kids home to their mother." Althea seemed anxious.

"Mommy's not home." Carlton added before Carl or Craig could say anything.

Althea's head quickly whipped around to look at Carl. "How do you know Carlton when you are here."

"She's been working a lot lately." Carl tried to cover.

"She's never home when we get home." Tianna answered for her brother.

"Huh, I *wonder* why?" The sarcasm was thick in Althea's voice.

"Come on guys. Give Grandma a kiss." Carl was suddenly ready to go and find out if his wife was at home.

"Jessi, you wanted Craig to yourself and now you can have him." Althea walked over to where Jessica sat. She looked as if she were going to pick her up out of the chair.

"Yeah, come on Jess."

He did not have to tell her twice. Jessica was standing at the door with Prada bag in hand before Craig could get the words out of his mouth. She smiled politely at Mr. Tillman and said good night. When she was outside the door, Jessica bent down to hug Carlton and Tianna.

"I'm gonna see if your mother will let me take you up on that golf offer."

Mr. Tillman seemed persistent. "Craig, do you play also?"

"I sure do. Just let us know and it will be the three of us. We've tried to teach mom how to play, but she's not interested." Craig cut his eyes over to his mother who looked like she was about to burst.

"Golf won't work for Thea since she doesn't like the sun." Mr. Tillman spoke as if he'd known Althea for years.

The brothers looked at each other in surprise.

"They know that, Adam. Don't let Craig pull your strings." Althea looked over at Mr. Tillman. "Bye, babies, Grandma loves you." The attention was back on the kids.

"Bye, Grandma." They sung.

"Alright Mom, I can take a hint." Carl said walking through the door.

Craig was behind him. "I'll call you when I get home, Mother."

"Ok, you all be careful." Althea said before closing the door.

The brothers stood on their mother's front porch in bewilderment.

"What just happened?" Craig broke the silence.

"Your mother just threw us out like yesterday's trash, so let's go." Jessica spoke matter of factly.

CHAPTER THIRTY-EIGHT

Tia was surprised to see that Ken was already in the office when she got there. She went into his office to find him with a blueprint spread out on the large conference table and Anthony Hamilton's "So in Love" pumping through the speakers throughout the office. "Well good morning, you're here early. What's going on?"

"What's up, T? I'm glad you're here. I've been waiting to show you the plans for my crib."

"Plans for your crib? What?" Tia asked as she walked over to the table.

"I've been looking since things are going so well with Lacey. I wanted —"

"Wow." Tia interrupted. "I can never understand blueprints, but this looks massive."

"Yeah, it's pretty big. Her mom is going to be with us, so we need the space. I wanted something with a guest house, but I think this could work."

"Whoa. You going from zero to a hundred real quick. Last month you were a bachelor and now you're looking at floor plans for you, your baby, your 'baby momma' *and* her momma."

They both laughed.

"Who would have thought that *you* would have a 'baby momma'? "

"You know that's not me, T. When I hear you say it, it becomes even more certain. I'm gonna ask Lacey to marry me."

Tia dropped down into one of the leather chairs that Ken had pulled out from the table so he could get closer. She was genuinely shocked by Ken's statement.

"What? T, you know me. I cannot have the mother of my child out here being called a 'baby momma'. Plus, I'm in love with Lacey. I don't know if things would have progressed the way that they have if she wasn't pregnant, but things have really changed for both of us now. "

"Wow, that's great, Ken." Tia was speaking slowly. She felt something and it almost felt like jealousy. "Pregnancies have been known to change things."

"I'm doing two masters; one up and one down so we can have our separate space if needed. Now I'm trying to figure out where to put the playroom because I don't know if Lacey would want us to use the upstairs or the downstairs bedroom."

"What is she saying?"

"About what? She doesn't know about the house. We've talked about living together, but I think she expects me to move into her place."

"She's got a lot to learn about her 'baby daddy'." Tia stood as she laughed. "You're a distraction today, Boss. My plan was to come in and take care of some things to make sure the projections are ready for the meeting on Monday. I need to get out of here at a reasonable time because Zena's in town."

Ken's face lit up. "I didn't know Zena was here."

"Yes, and it has been non-stop. I thought I would have a chance to clear my head and re-group, but it doesn't look like that will be happening."

"Sorry, T, but that's in your job description. I *know* I added the part about you being my listening ear, shoulder to cry on and problem solver." Ken was joking about it being in her job description, but he did depend on Tia for all the above.

"I think I need a raise." She turned to walk out.

"What you two getting into tonight?" Ken and Zena weren't as close as he and Tia, but they were all friends and the three of them always had a great time together. "I would love to see Z."

"She wants to see you too. She was just as surprised as everyone else when she heard the news. She can't wait to meet Lacey. Maybe we can arrange something."

"Great, let me know. Lacey hasn't been out of the house, so that may be a good reason for her to put some clothes on."

"Why, is she sick?"

"Not really. I think it's just a lot for her. She's used to being Ms. Independent, now she has me there doing my thing. She thought she was going to be a single mom and that ain't happening. Her hormones are raging."

"We'll see what happens. Rick scooped Zena up and I haven't seen her since."

"Slick Rick? He's still in the picture?

"He's trying. You know how that goes." Tia finally was able to escape and get to her desk.

As soon as she sat down, she could hear her cell phone ringing in her purse. It was Sean. "Good morning." She answered.

"Hey, you, I thought I would have heard from you by now. You busy?"

"Nope." Tia lied. "What's up?"

"Nothing really. I've just been thinking about you and couldn't understand why you never called me back yesterday. I know your girl's in town but I didn't expect you to forget all about me."

"Forget about you? Yeah, right. Zena is still M.I.A. I haven't even heard from her, but I had company and I was exhausted by the time they left. However, I did go to bed with you on the brain even though I wasn't able to call." Tia could not figure out why she smiled whenever she spoke to Sean on the phone. She was sure he could hear it.

"You went to bed with me on the brain, huh? I won't even respond to that."

"Yep, I did."

"Like I said, I'm not going to respond, at least not right now. I'll just toss that around in my mind for a while."

"Well, you do that."

"I was really calling to see if I could get a date with you guys later." "You...guys?" Tia spoke slowly just to be a tease.

"Yeah, you and Z, I enjoyed hanging out the other night. I had hoped to see you again over the weekend, but I guess it wasn't in the cards.

"I'm not sure if Zena will be back today. I want to give her space to do her thing, so I haven't even called."

"You haven't checked on her? What if something happened?"

"Trust me, Rick knows better. She's fine; she may be in La La Land, but that's nothing I haven't seen before."

"Women are funny. Why can't you be happy for your friend when she's happy? I don't see anything wrong with being in La La Land."

Tia thought that funny. She couldn't stop laughing because Zena probably was thinking that *she* was the one in La La Land.

"Really, whenever I hear women talk about their friends being in love or happy in a relationship, it's the La La Land thing or '*she's gone*'. I didn't expect that from you, Baby" Sean's voice softened at the end. "You know what? You may be right. Maybe I do go hard on Z with Rick, but it's because I was there when he hurt her. I was almost as devastated as she was, but you're making me sound like a hater."

"You're making me sound like a hater." Sean laughed. "Zena's a big girl. If she decides to give it another go, you should trust her judgement."

Wow, Tia thought, *that makes so much sense.* She didn't know what it was, but Sean could make the simplest thing seem profound. "Did she put you up to this?"

"Who?"

"Zena, you sound like you're representing her."

"I'm looking out for you, Baby. I'm trying to help you to see things more clearly. Think about it. Yeah, dude may have messed up, but no matter how devastated you say you were; you were *not* in that relationship. Zena is very intelligent, and she doesn't seem like the type to allow someone to mistreat *or* misuse her. So, trust that. And I'm sure she feels your side eye, where Rick is concerned, and she probably doesn't like it."

"Okay, it's jump on Tia day, and no one even told me."

"Alright, alright, what are you doing later? Let's grab a drink. If Zena turns up, she's welcome to come. If not, forget it."

"Forget it?" Tia was confused.

"I'm kidding. If she's back, cool. If not, it's just the two of us."

"Let me call you after lunch." Tia was getting flustered.

"Are you serious? I have to wait for an answer? Sean had wanted to see Tia all weekend. He didn't want to leave her Friday night after they had all gone out. He was disappointed that she didn't seem to feel the same. "I woke up with 1000 things on my mind. I came to work to clear my head and found Ken here before me. He unloaded his issues on me. Now, you're telling me I'm a hater, something that I have never been accused of before, Zena's missing, and I haven't done even five minutes of work. Yes, you do have to wait for an answer." She was smiling again.

"Well, I will be waiting for your call, Baby. I didn't mean any harm by what I said you know that, right?"

"What you said was right, Sean." She was not talking about the part about being a hater, but he was on point with the other things he said. "I'm cool."

"Okay. Try to enjoy your morning and I'll be waiting to hear from you."

"Bye." Tia hung up the phone and started typing a text to Sean.

I don't know if Z will be back, but the answer is YES. Let me know where and I will be there.

She pressed send. Tia did not know why, but she was smiling again.

CHAPTER THIRTY-NINE

The phone vibrated before Sean could set it on the desk. He was surprised to see a text from Tia. They were just on the phone. He couldn't help but smile when he read the text. He didn't respond right away because he didn't have a place in mind. He would take some time to think about it and give her a call later. He hoped she would be in a better mood by the time he spoke to her again.

Sean had literally been thinking about Tia ever since they parted on Friday night. At first it was because he knew that her and Zena were tipsy, and he was concerned about them making it home after they ran him off for getting too close to her home. However, he had stayed on the phone until she was safely in her driveway. Sean could still smell Tia's perfume when he reached home. He decided not to shower, so he went to bed with Tia's scent, and her, on his mind. Saturday morning Sean awoke with thoughts of the night before flashing through his brain. He was disappointed when he could no longer smell Tia's scent, and realized that Tia had been on his mind all night. He knew it was too early to call her, but he wanted to. He felt better when he thought about the day ahead of him. He would be busy so maybe he would not think about spending more time with Tia.

He pulled himself out of bed and knew that his parents would be expecting him soon. The first phase of his latest project was finished, and his parents enjoyed coming out to see how people react. He had hoped that Olivia would take them, but she was busy. She, like Sean, could not understand what his parents got out of sitting around watching other people's excitement. The phone rang and Sean knew that it was his parents calling to rush him along. "Hello."

"Good morning, baby, how are you? "

"I'm fine, Mother. How are you?"

"Are you sure? You don't sound fine."

"Well, I wanted to sleep in, but I knew that you or Dad would be calling soon."

"I wanted to make sure that you were up. You know how impatient your father can get. He's really looking forward to seeing the place. He said that his buddies have been talking about how grand it looks."

"Well, you can both relax. I'm up and getting ready. I will call you when

I'm on my way."

"Are the kids coming?"

"No, Mother, they've been there with me enough. They don't want to spend a Saturday there. We don't understand why you all want to go. I can take you there any time without all the fuss."

"Well, we like the fuss. Tell those kids that they are going to have to come over and spend the day with us."

"I sure will, and I'll see you shortly."

Sean disconnected the call and thought about how blessed his was to have both of his parents alive, still together, and with all their faculties. He would have to make the children go spend time with them. They hadn't done that in a while.

He showered, got dressed and thought about the evening he had with

Tia and Zena all the way to his parents' house. They were outside when Sean turned into the circular driveway. Sean shook his head and hoped that he would have better things to do when he reached their age.

Sean had to admit that his parents were pretty jazzy. They were both well-kept. They got into the Mercedes looking and smelling great.

"Hey Son, we thought you weren't coming."

"Hi, baby." Sean's mother was always happy to see her son.

"Hey, Mom."

"I know Mom told you that I said to relax, Pop. I had a long night last night."

"Before such a busy day?" Sean's father was concerned.

"I'm always busy, but I don't expect today to be bad. I was extremely busy in the beginning, but we've completed phase one now. I'm just going to make sure that the place is packed, and everything looks good.
"

"I can't believe your sister isn't coming." Sean's parents enjoyed doing things together as a family.

"She has plans today, Mom. It *is* Saturday you know. Besides, she was there with me the other night. She actually helped me out with the planning of the open house."

"If it was something that important, I don't think it would have been scheduled for Saturday." She quickly responded.

Sean just drove on, smiling to himself. He knew that his parents did not understand today's lifestyles and it was no use trying to get them to understand. He totally understood why Olivia opted out. He turned to the jazz station on XM Radio and the sound of the saxophone took his mind right to Tia. He thought about the way she swayed to the music the live band played the night before. He imagined being at an outdoor venue with her listening to some Brian Culbertson. He decided that he would check out some of the line ups for the summer Jazz Fests that were being planned around the country. Sean had thought about taking a trip with Tia before; he knew that it would be nice. He shook his head to come back to reality and it was not missed by his mother.

"Did you forget something, Sean?" His mother's concern came through in her voice.

"No."

"What's the matter?" She asked.

"Nothing's wrong, Mom. I'm just trying to stay focused that's all."

In his mind, Sean shook his head. If he really shook it, he knew that his mother would have noticed. Sean's mother knew him better than anyone because she always paid attention to what he was doing or saying. If he thought about something and a frown appeared on his face, his mother would be there to say...'what happened', or 'what's the matter'. It would not go unnoticed in his mother's presence and Sean took comfort in the way his mother doted over him and his sister.

Both of Sean's parents made a fuss when the car turned, and they were able to see The Acreage as they approached. Although Sean knew that the development was beautiful and it looked gorgeous from afar, he had turned that corner so many times that the view no longer caught him off guard. Sean's first couple of projects were with a partner, but this was the fifth development that Sean had done by himself. It was his most prestigious project, it was the most difficult to put together and Sean had prepared himself for the magnificence and fanfare. Of course, he was extremely proud of what he had done, but he made a point to keep it in the proper perspective.

As they got out at the welcome center Sean noticed the staff was busy adding the final touches. He had to admit that everything looked nice. It smelled delicious with pots of coffee brewing and cookies being baked. The pillows on the couches were fluffed to perfection and the windows were so clear that Sean was sure that a bird would fly right into one of them. The hostesses were beautiful and dressed to perfection. Sean made sure that his parents were comfortable and told one of the hostesses to look after them while he went to check the grounds. Before walking out, Sean looked at his parents and smiled seeing the proud look on both of their faces.

Sean jumped on one of the golf carts to take one last look around before people began to arrive. As he drove, there was nothing but beautiful homes and landscape for as far as his eyes could see and he admitted to himself that The Acreage was quite an accomplishment. He thanked God, again, for the wonderful blessing. He tried to stay focused but could not keep his thoughts from Tia. He wanted to share this accomplishment with her but knew that it would be totally inappropriate. Although, there were many days that he spoke to Tia about work and different issues that had come about, the conversations were never specific enough for him to say exactly what he was working on. Sean wondered if she had driven by or heard about the place. That made him smile;

knowing that she had probably heard about The Acreage. It was the current talk around town for the young and the old; anyone who was moving, or thinking, or knew someone that was thinking about moving was talking about The Acreage.

CHAPTER FORTY

Charles was impressed with Ken's enthusiasm. He had never seen him so excited about anything and he was thrilled and surprised with the floor plan that Ken had decided on. He didn't know how to break the news to Ken that the piece of land that he had his eye on was not a done deal. Charles had no idea that he would receive push back from the owners since Ken's initial offer was quite generous for the area. However, the property had been in the family for years and the owners had not heard the number that would make them sell. Ken had given Charles permission to negotiate the deal freely and Charles knew what the property was worth. He increased the offer 25K more and refused to go any higher. The owners didn't budge. Charles decided to back off for a while and let them think about the offer in hopes that they would come to their senses.

Ken discovered the vacant lot not far from where Lacey lived. He knew that he could get a better neighborhood and probably for less money, but he thought Lacey and her mother may have wanted to stay in the area. Charles warned him that it may take some time and some work to secure the location because it had been used as a commercial property for years. There was a storefront there years ago, which had since been demolished. Ken noticed it on the way to see Lacey and took note that it was neatly fenced and always clean and maintained. Ken mentioned the property to Lacey, in passing, to try to gauge how she felt about it. She said that it had been clean and well-kept ever since she moved to the area. She said that she always wondered who owned it and why it was still vacant.

"Man, I haven't seen you motivated like this since you opened the doors at Gama Global." Charles liked the drive in his little brother. He never understood Ken's complacency. Ken had turned down many opportunities to take Gama Global global which was the original plan.

It wasn't even that Ken was overwhelmed, but he was satisfied with the business that he was doing. "I think this baby may be the best thing that's happened to your ass. You've been needing some motivation."

"Please don't start coming at me about expanding Gama right now." Ken already knew how Charles felt about the company.

"Motivation is a good thing and that's all I'm sayin', Bro. Maybe Lacey and the baby will compel you to venture outside of your comfort zone."

"I'm sure they will, but you know I like to stay hands on when it comes to the business and that's all there is to it. Anyway, what's the word on the property?" Ken asked.

"Man, they aren't budging. I think they want more money."

"Seriously? In that neighborhood? I thought they would have jumped all over my offer."

"I know. I was hoping that you change your mind because I'm not gonna increase the offer again. What does Lacey think?"

"I don't really want to involve her that way." Ken confessed to his brother. "I'm hoping to surprise her."

"What? You got me pulling my hair out about this deal, and Lacey hasn't even agreed on the location?" Charles felt more relief than anything else. There was a chance that Lacey may not want to stay in the neighborhood. It was older, although it was nice and well-kept. The homes in the area were modest and what Ken was building may be a bit extreme for the area.

"It's her and her mother so I didn't want to take them out of the area.

You know since it's a surprise and all."

"You may want to think about that. With the money that you're about to spend, you do not want to find out that they've been wanting to move across town for years. Here you go with that comfort zone shit again. You worried about her, and I doubt it would be a problem. You are *building* a crib for her and her mother. I really don't think she would be upset about an upgrade in location. I know I wouldn't." Charles laughed.

Ken joined in when he thought about it. He honestly didn't think that Lacey would be ungrateful, but he wanted the house and the surprise to be as close to what she would want as possible.

"Well, I'm gonna do some research and try another approach." Charles wanted to help if he could, but it would be ridiculous to pay almost double the value for that property. He refused to let Ken go that route. "I've been dealing with the owner's agent. I'll try to sidestep him and get to the owners. The agent may be trying to make a little money for himself."

"Do what you gotta do. I'm ready to get started." Ken felt the enthusiasm come back into his voice. He knew that when Charles wanted to, he could make things happen.

"Yo, I could have sworn I saw Tia over in Midtown the other night." Charles had forgotten to call Ken about it the next morning.

"Midtown? I doubt it. I don't even think she knows about Midtown.

She's never said anything about it."

"Man, I would have bet money that it was Tia. I was on my way to say something, but she was with a dude."

"Was it Carl, her husband?"

"No, Bro! That's why I didn't go over there."

"Nah, that wasn't T." Ken thought about Zena being in town but decided not to mention it to Charles.

"Well good, but she was lookin' good as hell if it was her." They both laughed.

CHAPTER FORTY-ONE

Zena was in awe from the moment Anicka opened the door and they entered the massive hallway. Beams of light from the light fixture were like a design on the walls of the spacious passageway. She turned to look at Rick and saw that he was just as impressed as she was. Anicka looked at the two of them and smiled with a sense of pride because she had gotten the desired response.

"The Franklin Corporation spared no expense with these models so prepare to be inspired." Anicka felt the need to prepare the couple for the opulence. "I've rearranged every room in my house since the models have been finished."

Just standing in the doorway of the home felt good to Zena. The high windows all around allowed the sun to fill the home giving it an airy feel. Zena looked around and thought about the surreal feeling that she was having. *Why did I bring my ass here?* Zena realized at that moment that she may not have been emotionally ready to go out and do couple's activities with Rick.

"Are there any children?" Zena heard the question and wondered how long she had been in a daze.

"We don't have any of our own yet, but we both enjoy spending time with nieces and nephews." Rick responded and began to walk farther into the enormous home.

"This is the formal dining area as you can see." Anicka did the sweep with her hand as she spoke.

Although Zena had always thought that formal dining rooms were a waste of space, she was ready to live with the one she was standing in.

One complete wall was glass. The windows extended from the floor to the vaulted ceiling. There was shading for the windows that was controlled by remote. "Come on Z, you know we would never eat in here." Rick was heading to where the huge television was mounted on the wall.

"I know, but it's beautiful." Zena responded. "I like how it's off to the side. It would be ni —"

"That's what I love about it also." Anicka interrupted. "It has pocket doors to close it off if you want." Anicka slid a glass panel out of the wall of the entrance.

"I was gonna say that it would be nice if we could close it off. I don't think it would be used often."

"You can choose glass, or any of the wood options for the doors."

Zena knew that she would choose wood. She liked the idea of having space for everyone to eat together on holidays and for dinner parties, but she would also like the idea of it being a hidden surprise.

"This is nice." Rick almost whispered as he walked into the large space and imagined himself on the sofa watching a game and Zena behind him in the kitchen making her magic.

Zena didn't know if Rick had heard anything that was said about the dining area. "Wow, it is." She agreed standing in the middle of the space looking around at all there was to take in. The kitchen and family room seemed to be one huge comfortable area for friends and family to hang out. The kitchen was huge and was equipped with all the latest kitchen appliances and gadgets. The island was topped with the shiniest marble that Zena had ever laid eyes on and was lined with six high back stools.

"Yes, this is great living space. I know you don't have kids yet, but when you do I think you will appreciate this area even more." Anicka walked over to the extra wide refrigerator and took out a pitcher of what looked like orange juice. She took a couple flutes and poured two glasses of mimosas. "I want to show you two a couple things and then I can give you some time to get to know the house if you like." Anicka handed them each a mimosa and began to walk out of the kitchen.

There was also an office and a full bath on the first floor, and both were beautifully designed and decorated. However, what Anicka wanted to show was the bonus room. She opened the mahogany double doors to the last room on the first floor and Rick and Zena's mouths both dropped.

The room seemed to be the length of the entire house. In the center of the room was a pool table that looked like a piece of art, sitting on an oversized, brightly colored, plush area rug. There were two flat screen TVs on opposite walls in the room.

Zena knew that Rick was sold. He loved playing pool. She enjoyed playing also, but she always found the pool halls or billiard rooms to be cheesy. She would get upset whenever Rick asked her to play pool with him because she didn't like the places he went to play.

"Babe." Rick reached back and pulled Zena closer with his arm hooked around her neck. "This is it right here."

"You must know him from somewhere." Zena jokingly spoke to Anicka.

"No, I don't think so." Anicka answered honestly.

"Well, you know his weakness. You may just have a buyer."

Anicka smiled. "I think most men enjoy a game of pool, but it's hard to find a nice place to shoot, so we resolved that problem." Anicka spoke as if it were her decision to add the bonus room and the pool table. "The table comes in a plethora of color and material options and is also available with a dining room table combination."

"I don't know if you're going to be able to get him out of here, but I wanted to show you all something upstairs and then I will leave you for a while." Anicka spoke to Zena while Rick admired the table.

"Rick, we're going upstairs." Zena tried to bring him back into the conversation before she turned to walk out.

"You can show me, and I'll show him." Zena was sold on the bonus room and the house itself. She felt her emotions beginning to percolate. *Why did I come here? Why did I come here with Rick? Would he move here with someone else? Does he know that I want to move back? What if I don't get the job?*

The ladies left the room and went upstairs where everything seemed just as nice as downstairs. Zena peeked into 3 bedrooms before Anicka escorted her into the massive master bedroom. It was beautiful and had a spacious sitting area which was decorated in ivory and gold as well as the rest of the bedroom and the bathroom. This was Zena's favorite spot in the house. The look was luxurious and rich without being extravagant. Being in that room made Zena feel some kinda way. She imagined living there with Rick, and her and Rick getting dressed in that elegant bedroom to go out for drinks. She wondered what was happening and if being with Rick and looking at homes, beautiful homes, was too much for her heart that was still healing. She thought she was really over the pain of that relationship until now. She could not understand what she was feeling. And she could not understand

Anicka! "I'm sorry. I didn't hear you."

"I just said that I knew you would like this room. I could see the two of you."

"Whoa!" Rick finally caught up. "We're gonna have to drag *her* out of here."

"I know." Anicka responded. "I was just saying to Zena that I could see the two of you here. This house seems like it was made for the two of you."

"I don't know if you're just saying that or if it's a selling technique, but I can see myself living in this house. I don't even need to see the other homes because this is it for me." said Zena.

"I am being honest with the two of you. I'm a people watcher and I think I know some things about you two as a couple just from being in your presence. I don't mean to sound cliché, but I can tell that you both like nice things. You both look nice and as a couple you look great.

You're sexy and you look like you love each other and enjoy making each other happy. Yes, I would love for you to buy the house, but if you don't I still stand behind the things that I just said about you. Now come on. I have one more thing to show you before I go." She walked over and opened a door between the two walk-in closets. "This is my favorite to show." Anicka smiled and waved the couple passed her to go before her.

The door opened to a narrow staircase. Zena went up first followed closely by Rick and Anicka. "Oh my! I do not believe this." Zena was truly caught off guard by the sauna that had a jacuzzi in the center. The room was circular; like being in a tower and everything was wooden. There was a circular bench surrounding the jacuzzi.

"This is crazy!" Rick spoke through his laughter. "Yo, I have never seen anything like this."

"I know." Anicka spoke proudly. "This design was just approved for the

Franklin Corporation. I think it's brilliant."

Zena was still trying to absorb the whole thing. "So, this can be used as a sauna *or* a jacuzzi room?"

"Yes, and it has a safety feature so the room will not operate as a sauna if the jacuzzi is uncovered."

"I was just wondering if it was safe to have so much heat in such a small area. I think I've recently heard of someone dying from being in a sauna for too long."

"Well, we have that covered also. The sauna will not operate for more than 45 minutes at a time. It automatically turns off for at least 45 minutes after each 45-minute session since it was determined that maximum benefits are reached at between 30-45 minutes in a sauna and adverse effects begin at about 60 minutes. Of course, you know that they cannot be operated at the same time."

Rick could not stop looking at the bubbling jacuzzi. He was trying to do the numbers in his head, but he knew that he was going to have to do some juggling to be comfortable in such an upscale area.

"I'm going to run back to the welcome center and give you guys some private time to talk and look around some more. Feel free to do what you like." Anicka had a smirk on her face when she spoke the last sentence. She hoped that her thoughts did not show on her face, but from the way she saw Rick look at Zena she knew that her expression had betrayed her. She knew what she would have done alone with her man in that house, and she could not help but imagine what these two would get into.

Chapter Forty-one

Carl was pleasantly surprised to see his mom's number come up on the caller ID, but she caught him by surprise with her request. "Hey baby, I know you're probably busy, but Tillman is here, and he thought that you and your brother were serious about the golf game."

"Who?"

"Adam. He keeps asking me to call you two to set it up. I told him that you were just making small talk."

Carl was taken aback. So, this Tillman guy, Adam, or whatever his name is, was at his mother's house again? Right now? "Actually, Craig and I are going to play a quick round this afternoon." Carl lied. Then he realized that this could be one of his mother's episodes and said, "Put him on the phone. I'll see if he's up for it."

"Hello there, Son. Your Mom says, you guys don't want to play with me." Mr. Tillman sounded pleasant enough.

"Hello, sir, my mom's a joker. How's she doing? Is everything okay?" Carl was fishing.

"Yes. She's great. We just came back from having coffee. I think she wants to get a little rest before we go to service this evening. Are you and your brother ready for me? I have my clubs in the car."

"I just told Mom that Craig and I are going to hit a round at The Point this afternoon. Can you make it?"

"I wouldn't miss it. What time?"

"How does 2:00 sound?" Carl gave himself time to track down Craig and get him there.

"2:00 tee time, I'll see you then. Thea..." Tillman found Althea and handed her the phone back.

Carl's head was spinning. 'Thea?' He could not wait to talk to Craig.

"You two, please behave, and send Adam back here in one piece, okay?" Althea was tired and needed a nap.

Carl could not end the call fast enough. "Craig, get your clubs and meet me at The Point at 2:00." That was the voice message that he left on his brother's voicemail before deciding to send the same thing in a text message.

Craig looked across at Jessica's shocked face. When she saw him walk into her office with the extra-large Louis Vuitton bag, she must have thought he was coming with a gift for her.

He had decided that Jessica may not be a good fit for him and his family. Because of his mother's illness, Craig felt that he needed more time to be available for her. He was also uncomfortable with the way Jessica openly displayed her frustrations concerning Althea. He looked around his house the night before and found that Jessica had strategically left her belongings throughout his house. There was a nightgown behind the bathroom door of the guest bathroom. Craig never knew that Jessica even went into that part of his house. When he found the sundress and suit hanging in the guest bedroom, he could not let it go. He wondered if she was trying to move in on him or if she was just being territorial. Whatever it was, he did not like it. He had once considered something serious with Jessica, but things had changed…quickly.

He asked Jessica if those were her clothes in the guest bedroom, although he knew they were. He wanted to know why she never said anything and why she didn't leave them in his bedroom, where they slept whenever she stayed over. Her response of "What's the big deal?" was the decision maker.

He started a pile with everything that he could find that belonged to Jessica and it ended up being much larger than Craig imagined, hence the extra-large Louis Vuitton bag that her things were packed into. When he walked into her office, Jessica's face lit up. *Is she happy to see me or is it the bag I'm holding?* Craig thought to himself. He didn't immediately hand it over but gave her the usual hug and kiss on the lips. He sat at her desk and asked how her day was going.

"Better now." Jessica flashed a smile at Craig. "I'm actually pleasantly surprised."

Craig took both of Jessica's hands and held them in his when he began speaking. "Jess, I need to fall back for a minute." *Not a good beginning,* Craig thought when he saw the look on Jessica's face. He didn't know where those words came from. "I'm sorry. I never expected to have to do this or say this, but I have so many things going on right now. I just don't think I can be the man you need the way that I'm being pulled in so many directions. My mom's health is constantly on my mind. I'm always thinking of what else I can do."

"There's nothing for you to do, Craig. It's not in your hands." Jessica spoke as if Althea was in Hospice or something.

Jessica's crass reply made things much easier for Craig. "What do you mean, there's nothing that I can do? That's my mother Jessica." Her flippant responses got to Craig, especially when they involved his mother. "Even when there is nothing that I can do, I'll still want to do more. I know…I see that you don't really understand my position here, which is why I started thinking that you don't deserve to be in this conundrum that I'm in right now. You deserve the unbridled happiness that I can't offer to you at this time." *Is that clear?* Craig questioned himself. "I basically want you to have your freedom to move around and see what's out there for you."

"So, you buy me a gift to make it better?" Jessica was confused.

The frown on Craig's face revealed his confusion. "Huh? Oh, I'm sorry, the bag." Craig dropped the bomb. He picked up the bag and handed it to Jessica while saying, "I put all of your things that I've found around my house in here. I'm pretty sure everything's there, but if anything's missing just let me know." Craig was glad to be interrupted by his phone ringing. He picked it up to look and see that Carl was calling. *I'll call him when I leave,* Craig thought and sat the phone back on Jessica's desk.

Jessica opened the bag, just a little, as if she were hoping to see something wrapped in caramel colored tissue inside. She was disappointed to find her own clothes really were inside.

Craig quickly picked the phone back up when he heard the text notification. 'Get your clubs and meet me at The Point at 2:00', Carl's text read. *That was strange,* Craig thought to himself, maybe he forgot to mention it last night. It was 1:00 already, so he had to run. "That's Carl, he wants to meet. I've gotta run." Craig stood. He felt uncomfortable being so abrupt but didn't want to let the relationship linger any longer. He knew it had become a waste of time.

CHAPTER FORTY-TWO

Ken heard the music that was coming from Tia's office stop. He heard papers shuffling and he heard keys, so he knew that it was way past the 4:00 cutoff time that he scheduled for himself today and he knew Tia was leaving. He had not forgotten about Zena and was surprised that Tia stayed as late as she had.

"Good night, boss." Tia was walking quickly so Ken would not stop her. She hadn't planned to be there so late. Zena had called to say that Rick dropped her by her mom's, and she would wait there for Tia to pick her up after work. Tia was exhausted and thought that maybe they could make some drinks at the house, talk and chill for the evening. Ken could swing by with Lacey if he wanted. The twins hadn't seen him in a while and would be thrilled to know that Uncle Ken was having a baby. Tia smiled. She was happy to see that Ken seemed happy, more than happy actually. He was displaying the same *I'm gonna be the best father that the world ever saw* attitude that Carl had years ago when they found out that she was pregnant.

Tia pulled up at Zena's parents' house and was reminded of the many days that they sat on her front porch making plans. They sat there and designed their prom dresses and talked about boys and colleges. She laughed when she thought about how far they had come together. That front porch is where Tia first showed Z her engagement ring. That front porch is where Tia met Rick for the first time, and that front porch is where Zena told Tia about Rick and Eva. *It was the best of times, it was the worst of times, it was the age of wisdom, and it was the age of foolishness… No truer words,* Tia thought to herself right before Zena's mother swung the front door open. "Tia!" She had her arms stretched wide and Tia walked into her embrace. "I told you that Zena does not have to be here for you to stop by. I should at least see you when I can't see her. And you're pretty as ever. Where are the babies? Zena's been talking about how big they've gotten."

Tia felt the love when she walked in. "I'm coming, T." Zena yelled from upstairs.

"No rush." Tia replied. "You know I'm about to go in here and see what your mom is cooking."

"Come on. I made a salad when Z told me you were coming, because I know you are not gonna eat what I cooked for Wilson." She went and pulled a fully loaded salad out of her refrigerator. Wilson was Zena's dad, who was sitting in the den where he always was after work. He owned a heating and cooling company but stayed out just as late as his workers did every day. Then he came home, sat in the den and waited for his dinner to be served. He would eat while watching the news, then he was off to bed, and it had been that way for nearly 30 years.

"That salad does not look like it was impromptu." Tia said, but she was tipping around the corner to sneak up on Wilson. "Mr. Wil!" Tia stood in the doorway smiling as if she were surprising her own father.

Wilson turned to Tia and his face lit up. "Gina! Where have you been?

I've been worried. I've been waiting for you to come see me."

"That's not Gina, Will. That's Tia." Zena's mom grabbed Tia's wrist and pulled her in front of Wilson so he could see her better.

Tia leaned in to hug him. "Mr. Wil, I know you didn't forget about me."

Wilson hugged Tia tightly. "Of course not Tia. How are you?" He could not hide the disappointment in his voice, but he was happy to see Tia.

"I've always told my wife and Zena that you remind me of my niece

Gina, but today, you're looking just like her."

Zena walked in with perfect timing to chime in with her mom. "He always says that." The two of them spoke in unison.

"They do favor, Z." Her mother reiterated.

Zena walked over to give Tia a hug and whispered, "She just crazy though."

Mrs. Shorter could not possibly have heard Zena, but she felt the need to explain. The three ladies moseyed back to the kitchen while Mrs. Shorter spoke. "That was his sister's only child and Will thinks that he's the only family the girl had."

"She's married, with kids and she knows where we are." Zena interrupted her mother.

"Zena! Stop it." Her mother was firm. "He's been by to try to see her a couple times and no one ever answers the door. The housekeeper used to answer the bell and tell him that she was sleeping or out, but he says he gets no answer at all now."

"Daddy doesn't even know her, Mom." Zena sounded frustrated. "He's closer to Tia than he is to her, and that's his niece. I just don't like him sitting here worrying about her and she does not have the decency to even let him know that she is still alive. And she knows that we want to see the kids even if we don't see her. You cannot tell me that this is all because of her husband."

"I'm sorry T." Mrs. Shorter said. "This is Zena's older cousin. She's always been distant, but –"

"She married some rich man and forgot about her real family." Zena blurted out. "She moved her mother in with them, behind some iron gate."

"Girl shhhhh!" Mrs. Shorter snapped. "We don't know what happened and we may never know. All we do know is that her mother passed, and she had somewhat of a nervous breakdown. We haven't seen her since the funeral."

"He drove her ass crazy; that's what happened." Zena did not mean to let the curse word slip out.

"Somebody must be driving you crazy if you think you can talk that way in here." Mrs. Shorter shot.

"I'm sorry, Mom, but you know I have never liked the way they treated

Dad. He's always ran behind them, even when auntie was alive."

"That was his little sister, Z, you know your father is a protector." Zena noticed the confused look on Tia's face. "I know you remember me talking about my cousin, Gina, who thought she hit the lotto when she married this developer. The family was all happy for her until she got married and did a 180 on us."

"Yes, I remember. I remember that I wanted to go to the wedding with you, but it was super private or something. I thought she moved away.

You haven't mentioned her in years."

"Girl, you see why…"

Mrs. Shorter had set out a mini spread while they were talking, and she had snapper filets coming out of the grease. *How did she have every salad topping and a selection of salad dressings in her refrigerator,* Tia thought. *I always have to go to the store and get croutons or something.* Everything they wanted was on the table in front of them.

Chapter Forty-three

Ken could not stop thinking about the house. Maybe Charles was right about Lacey being open to moving to a new area. He knew that she was unsure about the stability of their relationship because things were happening so fast. They went from dating, to being friends with benefits and now they are about to be parents. *She must want more,* Ken thought as he watched her getting ready. She looked happy; happier than he has seen her since she had given him the news. Ken walked up behind Lacey and heard her humming. "What's up with you?" Ken asked. "Are you that happy to be getting out of the house?" He was almost serious because he did not see this change in attitude coming.

Lacey was still wrapped in her towel from the shower, and she turned around to face Ken. She had already put her makeup on and had a huge smile on her face. She threw her arms up in the air and said, "I'm having a baby!"

That exclamation and the joy in Lacey's face, made Ken's eyes well up with tears. He picked her up so that her face was right in front of his, he knew that he was squeezing her tight and hoped that he wasn't hurting her. Ken tried to match Lacey's enthusiasm when he said, "We're having a baby!" He carried Lacey and laid her on her bed as gently as possible. Both of their faces were wet with tears when he went to kiss her.

Lacey kissed the tears that rolled down Ken's face. "I am soooo scared,

Ken. But I am so happy that you are on this journey with me."

He didn't know what to say or do. Ken was so full of emotion, of love that he felt that he was going to burst. He tried to explain his feelings to Lacey. He told her that she was the perfect person for him to have a child with. That no one else would do. However, his words were not adequate enough to express what he was feeling. Ken didn't even think his plan all the way through before he was pulling Lacey's arms so that she was sitting all the way up. Her towel had fallen on the bed and her breasts looked swollen and beautiful. When Lacey was sitting upright, Ken slid to floor and on one knee said, "Lacey, I love you. I want to spend the rest of my life with you. Will you marry me?"

Lacey was stunned. She stared down into the watery eyes of her child's father, speechless; then the tears began to flow. She held Ken's wet face, and placed slow, sloppy kisses on Ken's nose, cheeks, and lips. Between sniffles and stares, Lacey managed to say, "I love you so much.

Of course, I will marry you."

The couple held each other and cried for a while before Ken said, "I don't have your ring...yet." Ken threw the 'yet' in as not to alarm Lacey. "I didn't plan on proposing to you...today" He stumbled. Ken could not believe that he couldn't get his wording together. He was trying to be as transparent as possible with his future wife. "I just want you to know that I'm here for you...from now on. You don't have to ever be afraid, Lace. I'm here...it's us now." That was from the heart, and Ken hoped that Lacey felt the sincerity. "I wanted Tia to come with me to help me pick out a ring for you, but now you can pick your ring…if you want to." Ken didn't know if picking your own ring was tacky or not. "I haven't asked Tia yet, but I'm pretty sure I'll end up spending a lot more money with her picking." It was the truth. Ken knew that Lacey would choose something nice but conservative, because that's the person that she is, and Tia would choose something beautiful but pricey, because that's the person that she is.

"What? Tia doesn't know? I'm surprised." Lacey knew how close Tia and Ken were. She loved Tia but was also relieved to know that Tia is happily married. She would not want a single woman like Tia that close to her man.

"Oh, she knows about the proposal. She just did not know that I wanted her to help choose your ring. She's excited and has already claimed her spot as the God mom." Ken didn't think that Lacey had anyone in mind because she never really hung out with any girlfriends that he knew of, and she rarely spoke about family. "I hope you don't mind. We can always have two sets of Godparents anyway, but Tia is the closest thing to an auntie that our baby will ever have from my side. Does your mom have sisters?" Ken needed to know more about the family that he was about to marry into.

"Yes, she does. I guess you will get to meet your future in-laws soon." Lacey liked the way the words sounded rolling from her lips. "I don't know how that's going to work out, but my uncle has visited us a couple of times. He's buying a place in The Acreage, so I'll speak to him to see how we can work things out. I think it will be good for Mom to see the rest of her family. It's been years."

Ken's wheels were turning. He knew that it would be at least a year before they would move into their dream home…realistically. Maybe, now he would bring Lacey in on his plan to build and get her thoughts on locations. "The Acreage? Where is that?" Ken hoped it was nearby. It would be nice for Lacey to have family members close.

"The massive development they've been working on for the last year; the one that you see when you're on 75." Lacey's uncle had taken her to see the place when he was in town. They were still working on it, but it was beautiful. Even the smallest home was elaborate. The grounds even had two towers of luxury condos, which is what Lacey's uncle bought. The place was like a little city that was secluded from everything else around. Although, everything anyone could possibly want, or need was right outside the iron gate that surrounded the entire property. The iron gate and the guard's station made the place seem even more exclusive than it probably was.

"Oh, it's called The Acreage? I forgot all about that place, it's huge." Ken hadn't been by there in a while but remembered how nice it was the last time he had passed it.

"I think each house is on an acre. My uncle is only buying one of the condos to try to get closer to mom." Lacey loved her uncle. She couldn't understand why he was single but knew that he would not be on the market long once he moved in town.

"Is it close? I don't remember exactly where it is." Ken started moving.

He wanted a better look at The Acreage.

"It's not too far away, maybe a fifteen-minute drive." Lacey thought it was a great location for her uncle. The condo had two bedrooms in case her mom wanted to stay with him sometimes, her uncle had told her. He and her mom were really close growing up. He always felt that he should have been there for her when she first got started with the drugs. He was staying with one of his many girlfriends at the time.

"Hey, are you still up to run over to Tia and Carl's? I want to go before it gets too late. I think Zena leaves tomorrow."

"Yep, I want to put some clothes on and go outside like a regular person. I have not been out of this house."

"I know. I was hoping that you were going to stay inside for the entire pregnancy." Ken was making light of it, but he didn't know what he was dealing with. Lacey had done a lot of crying. He was happy to see that she was starting to feel better. "Hey what about the ring? You want to be in on it?" It honestly didn't matter to Ken.

Tia threw the door open and was happy to see the glow on Lacey's face. "Come in." She hugged Lacey enthusiastically and walked the two of them to the back where Zena was pouring the last of their second bottle of wine in the two glasses. "Look who came to see you, Z!" Tia was standing behind Ken guiding him towards Zena.

"Aaaaaahhhhh! I was coming to look for your ass!" Zena screamed, and wrapped her arms around Ken's neck as if he were her long lost brother.

"No, I'm gonna fly across the country to help you pack and come back home." Ken spoke in Zena's ear as he picked her up and turned her around lovingly. He put Zena's feet on the floor and looked at Lacey and Tia smiling as if they had just seen a lost puppy returned to an owner. "I'm sorry, Babe." Ken grabbed Lacey's hand. "You've heard us talk about Zena." He knew she remembered he and Tia cracking up laughing about something Zena had said or done. "We go

waaay back." Ken said. "And Z, this is Lacey…my fiancé."
Ken could see Tia's face and her mouth when it dropped
open.

CHAPTER FORTY-FOUR

Carl was happy to see Craig pull up a few minutes early. He wasn't sure that he had gotten his messages. He started walking towards him so he could quickly let him know what happened and why they were there. After his update, both brothers thought that they needed to know more about this Adam Tillman and how long he had been hanging around their mother.

Obviously, neither of them remembered how their mother's friend looked because he walked right up to them unnoticed. "Hey guys." Tillman walked and put a hand on Carl's shoulder. "I thought you two would be on the green already."

"Hey, man, how's it going?" Carl responded and the startled brothers gave him the handshake with the little hug at the end. "We were hoping to talk to you before we started." Carl hadn't noticed how tall Tillman was the other day. He was quite handsome, Carl realized, and he looked very well-kept. His skin was bright, his nails looked freshly manicured, and he was wearing Dunning. For some reason, Carl started to feel better.

"How are you, Mr. Tillman?" Craig could not forget this man's name. He had thought about him since they met at

Althea's. He showed up on Google as a community leader, although Craig had never heard of him.

"Call me Adam please." He spoke with a casual tone as they walked towards the clubhouse. "Good idea to sit first. I've been wanting to speak to the two of you, but your mother has been doing a good job of running interference."

"What are you drinking?" Craig asked Adam when they got inside. He knew that Carl wanted water and so did he. Craig hadn't paid much attention to Adam the other day at his mom's, but he was a goodlooking man; tall, and looked to be in good shape. *He must have always been athletic,* Craig thought as he waited for an answer.

"I'll have a water. Thank you."

Carl decided to start the conversation, because he didn't want Craig to come off as a protective father. He thought that he could be a little more diplomatic when trying to find out just how well this man knew their mother. "So, mom never told us about you." Carl paused.

Tillman said nothing but looked directly at Carl.

"And we were a little surprised to meet you." Craig walked up with three bottled waters.

"I was a lot surprised to meet you to be honest, Mr. Till…Adam. My mom's been kind of sick lately. She hasn't really been herself."

"Sick?" Adam sounded surprised. "She told me that she had some testing, but sick? When?" She never mentioned to him that she wasn't feeling well. She told him that she had been more tired than usual, but not sick.

"I wouldn't say sick, Craig. She said that she was tired, so she took herself to the hospital."

"She took herself to the hospital…" Adam's bright eyes dropped. His concern was apparent.

"Yes." Craig continued. "They did some tests that came back inconclusive, so we're just keeping a closer eye on her for now."

"So, you must understand how we feel. We just want to keep our mother as safe as possible." Craig wanted to get to it. "Please, don't get me wrong, but Mom normally tells us everything and it was a surprise to see you in her home. It was obvious that you had been there before…you knew my niece and nephew."

"So, I guess what we want to know is how long have you been friends? Maybe you could have given us a warning about her behavior."

"If we had known you two were friends." Craig chimed in.

Tillman understood, but was feeling bad that Althea had driven herself to the hospital. She knew that she could have called him. He lived only five minutes away from her. "Well, it sounds like we are all on the same page." He was speaking with strength. "I hadn't met your children before, Carl, but your mother talks about them constantly, and of course the pictures everywhere." He smiled when he thought about the way Althea's voice sounded when she spoke about Carlton and Tianna. "Thea seemed fine prior to going to the hospital that day. If I noticed anything strange, I would not have left her alone before she got checked out. She told me she had a bad day, and I believe that. I haven't seen any signs of Alzheimer's either." He was ready to be honest with the men. "I've known your mother for a few years. As she told you, we met in church. We've been spending time together for more than a year now. I think, no I'm sure that I would notice anything outside of the normal forgetfulness. Let's not forget that your mother and I are of a certain age." Tillman smiled.

"So, we may forget things from time to time. Actually, that brings me to my point." He had both men's attention now. "I bought a condo in The Acreage."

"Okay, I've heard it's nice over there." Craig spoke and Carl squinted in thought. "The grounds sure look nice I been planning to drive inside and check it out."

"Oh, the spot off 75, right? Everyone's been talking about it." Carl blurted. "They have condos?" Carl asked, he remembered admiring the place while driving by.

"You name it and they have it over there." Tillman spoke. "I got in early because the developer is the son of a good friend. I got a rather good deal." Tillman had gotten a *really* good deal from his nephew; Sean was really his fraternity brother's son, but Adam was there when he was born, at every graduation, and at most of his major life events.

Hell, he was probably somewhere close by when he was conceived.

Both men were impressed that Tillman was savvy enough to be one of the first to get a piece of real estate in one of the newest and hottest spots in the area but had no idea how it involved them.

Tillman knew the men were waiting for the punch line and he continued. "The Acreage is a 20-minute drive from your mother. I've checked it." He confirmed before anyone could interject. "I live 5 minutes from her already, and that seems to be too far. I want your mother to move to The Acreage with me."

CHAPTER FORTY-FIVE

Tia was sad as Carl put Zena's bags in the back of her SUV. She always disliked her friend's departures just as much as she enjoyed her arrivals. She hoped that she wasn't being selfish, but Tia really wanted Zena to move home. It seemed like Rick had left an impression because she could not stop talking about him on the ride. He had taken her to The Acreage, they had done a tour, and Z's mind was blown. She said the presentation was impeccable and went on and on about how beautiful their agent was and how she seduced them with the house. It almost sounded to Tia as if they had christened the place. She made a mental note to mention it to Sean. He's probably already been there, she thought, and she wondered again about where Sean lived.

"There was this fly, old couple in there. They made me think about you and Carl."

"What?" Tia smiled.

"I mean in 25-30 years or something." Zena laughed. "No hate though, they were very nice people. Well-kept and good looking…looked like they had a driver and all." Zena thought about the black car that came for the couple. "They may have owned the place." That had just occurred to her. She had the brochures in her lap still looking through them.

Tia thought about Carl. A year ago, she may have seen the vision that Zena saw of her and Carl 30 years later, but for some reason she could no longer conjure it up. Tia drove, and kept trying to envision what her marriage would look like in 30 years. She couldn't, so she shortened it to 20, then 15, then 10. She was able to collect a vision of her and Carl in 5 years at a crossroad. *That's scary,* Tia thought. Then she thought about Sean. *Was that my problem?* She thought, already knowing the answer. Tia knew that Sean was, at least, part of the problem.

"Earth to Tia." She heard Zena say as they pulled into the airport departures. "You have not heard a word that I said, Girl. It must be Sean on the brain again." Zena laughed while opening the door. She had been trying to tell Tia that she was correct. The older couple had told her and Rick that their last name was Franklin, and the developer is The Franklin Group. Tia was in another world and Zena understood. She had history with Carl and loved him dearly, but Sean was charming as hell.

Tia laughed and walked around to send Zena off with a hug. "Girl!" She held her friend tightly. Tia needed the hug from her friend. "He was trying to come to the airport with me. He told me to tell you that he may have to come up your way on business next week and he's gonna call you."

Zena looked puzzled. "No, Ma'am,"

"He asked if I mind, and you know I trust you." Tia felt funny because Sean was *just her friend*. She knew that she would have to deal with that situation, and soon. She needed to work it out in her own mind what she was doing. She had romantic feelings for another man, and that was a fact, but was she going to act on them? The alternative would be to forget she ever met Sean. "I love you! Call me when you land." Tia tried to dismiss Zena's turn down.

"I will, and I love you too, but I'm not doing it." Zena sang as she turned to roll her bag into the airport. "What's his last name anyway? I haven't done my standard Google search." She laughed but was not joking.

Tia laughed, and wondered why she hadn't done hers either. "Franklin, silly." Tia said as she got back into her car and watched Zena walk away...still trying to look at those damn brochures.

"To be Continued..."

www.ingramcontent.com/pod-product-compliance
Lightning Source LLC
Chambersburg PA
CBHW051128020726
47501CB00005B/1410